Poppy
The Stolen Family

by

Carol Jeanne Kennedy

Publication Rights

Cover: *Rose Potocka,* 1856 by Franz Xaver Winterhalter (German, 1805-1873.) Public domain.

Dedications

To all my wonderful friends and family who helped me along the way in writing my novels. This book is dedicated to Don Knight, Billy Miller, Jean Gess, Carol Silvis, and Mary Burdick. Also, special thanks to Hennie Bekker whose musical compositions *Algonquin Trails* and *Stormy Sunday* provided the creative spark for *Winthrope*, followed by the rest of my Victorian Collection.

Other Great Novels by this Author

Winthrope – *Tragedy to Triumph*
The Arrangement – *Love Prevails*
Bobbin's Journal – *Waif to Wealth*
Poppy – *The Stolen Family*
Sophie & Juliet – *Rags to Royalty*
The Spinster – *Worth the Wait*
Holybourne – *The Magic of a Child*
A Novel Victorian Cookbook – *Forgotten Gems*

Links and Reviews

Visit the author's website: KennedyLiterary.com
Like on Facebook: caroljeannekennedy
Follow on Twitter @carol823599

Table of Contents

Chapter 1 – Shoes for Lady Allenton

"Grace, take these shoes to Lady Allenton." Holding her aching back, Mama glanced out our tiny, grime-smudged window and winced. "And be quick about it."

"Yes, Mama."

"You know the way, then?"

"Oh, yes, Mama, we know the way." I sighed, petting Holly on the head. "We've been there many times. In the spring, his lordship always buys bunches of my flowers."

"I haven't the time to listen to your gibberish, hurry along now. There is much work to do before the clock strikes."

Mama's pale skin, bluish 'neath her dark eyes, usually cast yellowish tinges, but today a silvery pate spread beneath her black lashes. I took the shoes and hurried from the room. "Come, Holly, we shall take the short way to the Great House."

Being very little, no one ever noticed me as I squirmed in and around those on the walk. "Come along, Holly." She loved to scamper ahead sniffing every stain mark on the stones, but I knew not to linger and urged her to move ahead. We had to be home for the laundry. My chore was to climb atop the footstool and fetch the clothes from the pegs, tables and chairs, fold them neatly, being very careful to stack them in their proper bundles.

Mama had a plan, she always had a plan. It seemed at every stroke of the town clock she was always hurrying before the next one struck. One day it was laundry, the next cleaning shoes, the next repairing books, the next sweeping her street corner—in the spring we would sell flowers. I found it fortunate, indeed, to sell flowers, as I scurried alongside gentlemen, tugging on their waistcoats encouraging them to buy my flowers—and they did. Perhaps I reminded them of their own. But as many times, I felt as if I were a delicate flower of little consequence. I had no idea, but I sold very many daisies.

"Come along now Holly, we must hurry." I skipped along our gloomy dark alley; hopped over horse dung, house slop, and the gin-house drunkards as they slept off last evening's rout. I sang my way along most of these darker places in hopes a bucket of slop wouldn't be tossed out atop my head. Holly never got drenched, and I often wondered how she managed to avoid them. Dogs are really smart.

Just ahead was the gate, the back entrance to the townhouse where the Earl of Allenton lived with his ladyship—when they were in residence that is, which was seldom. I rather supposed they enjoyed their country home somewhere or the other, I think about twenty miles away. It was a very great distance. Lord Allenton once told me I could never walk there in one hundred years. One hundred years? Mama taught me to count numbers and read. She was once a teacher, someplace very far away, I rather supposed that as well.

"Come along, Holly, and this time you must stay close to me. You cannot run through the flowers anymore, the gardener will scold you again." I held the shoes close to my body, sniffing them. They smelled like Mama's hands. Not a scuff or cake of mud anywhere. "Her ladyship will be pleased."

Standing at the servants' entrance I wasn't tall enough to reach the bell-pull, so I turned the handle and let myself in. The cook never minded when I'd do that, but this morning the kitchen was unusually quiet. The floors hadn't been swept, the scrubsink window was cracked, and soot had found its way around the wash tub. "Hello," I called. "Hello." I tiptoed along the old stone floors in front of the cold blackened hearth and called out again. Still, no one answered. "Everyone is gone, Holly."

I wondered what I was supposed to do with the shoes. Surely I couldn't just put them on the table. Perhaps Mama was wrong? She did say take these shoes to Lady Allenton, I remember exactly. Hmm, I was just about to leave the kitchen when I heard someone cough. I followed the noise and along the way found that the house had been all shut up. The furniture was covered, the paintings turned, the tapers removed, the carpets rolled. But who was that I heard? Suddenly a very large man dressed in black carrying a book came around the corner and stopped. Removing his spectacles, he glared down at me. "What, little girl, may I ask are you doing in this house?"

"Ah," I stammered, "ah," I held up the shoes, "Mama told me to deliver these to Lady Allenton, sir."

"Well, you're a little late, they left days ago." He took the shoes and examined them, shaking his head. "Why, the heels are not even level."

"Level? Lady Allenton didn't want them level."

"Your mother, a cobbler? Well, it's a cobbler's job to not only clean them, but to see that the heels are not wobbly." He held them out for my inspection. "See here, little girl, look at the heels. Lady Allenton would certainly wobble about in these."

"Oh." I frowned examining them. "You are very right, sir." I glanced up at him. "I should take them back then."

"No, no, you won't." He sighed heavily as if put out by such a task. "I'll repair them myself, but you'll not get a penny for your work here, little girl … ah, what is your name?"

"Poppy, sir."

He smirked. "Poppy? What sort of name is that, pray tell?"

Poppy is my nickname, sir. It was given to me because of my red hair and the way I walked, springing about so. Indeed, I suppose I look like a flower. But Mama does not like the name …

"And your companion?"

"Holly, sir."

The man's face crinkled. "Holly?

"I found her hiding under a holly bush, just there, last summer. I pointed toward his lordship's garden. She was a stray."

"Very well, then." He gestured. "Hurry along, I am very busy and don't need to clean up after two vagabonds." His eyes cast down at the shoes. "And now to repair her ladyship's shoes, well, I will certainly remember to mention it to her."

I nodded. "Oh, yes, sir." I turned to leave the way I came in. "Good-bye, sir." We turned to leave.

"No, no, not that way." He pointed with a frown. "You must use the front entrance. The back gate has been locked."

"We came that way, sir."

He looked down into my face. "You came in from the alley, the back gate, through the garden then?" His brow furrowed with a question. "How did you get past that locked gate?"

"It was open, sir. I mean, it wasn't locked. I come that way all the time. When his lordship was about his garden there, he would buy my flowers."

"His lordship? Bought flowers? Flowers from you?" He shook his head, adjusting his spectacles with a tic. "Preposterous, little girl."

I stood fiddling with the folds in my apron, thinking of something to say.

"In the summer, his lordship would have had all the flowers he needed and surely would not have bought anything you might have had to sell. Why, his gardens are the most spectacular in all of London." He shook his finger at me, Holly growled.

"Shush, girl." I petted her head. "Well, sir, yes, but I am not telling fibs. He particularly loved my daisies ... the white ones. I remember very well that he did."

"Oh, I doubt that," he pooh-poohed pushing me toward the door. "Well, be on your way now, I am a very busy man."

"Yes, Mister ... ?

He shook his head. "Mr Cooke, not that you'll remember it. Now, you and your stray, be about some other mischief."

"Yes, Mr Cooke." Holly and I headed for the front entrance.

"And, miss, be sure and mention to your mother about Lady Allenton's heels." He shook his head mumbling as we left.

I *had* to mention Lady Allenton's shoes to Mama, for I left without a penny. I closed the massive front door behind me as Holly ran ahead sniffing this, sniffing that. I hadn't come this way before, but I was most certain Tuppence Lane was just ahead, to my left and then two streets more to where I had stood to sell my flowers in the spring.

Looking up, I noticed the clouds that had tumbled in—blackish, churning sort of rain clouds. "Come along, Holly. It will soon rain." Hurrying up Tuppence Lane we reached the avenue, but it did not look the same. Now it was raining hard, and I had not an umbrella. "Holly, come." We stood in the alcove of a glover's shop. Glancing in, I noticed the help lighting candles. I thought of Mama and the clothes hanging to dry. She would be taking them all in, but where would she hang them? It would be double work, for tomorrow not only did we have to sweep our corner, but we also had the clothes to iron.

I stood in the alcove looking up and down the street not at all sure just where I was. Bales of fog were now pushing in and around everything. I could hear the ships on the Thames blowing their loud thunderous blow horns, I could hear the clop-clop of carriage horses, faceless voices swishing past me, coming and going. The door behind me suddenly opened rudely pushing me off the steps.

"Be about some other place!" shouted a woman. "And don't be crowding the steps."

Now squinting up at her, I shouted into the blowing rain. "Excuse me, ma'am, I am not sure where I live." I wiped my eyes. "Do you know of ... ?"

Holding the door open, she shook her broom. "Get along, now! How should I know where you live?"

I gathered up Holly and hopped about the pools of rainwater, now swirling dungs of house slop and foamy slime of one sort

or the other. I knew standing in the street was a dangerous place
to be and made my way to the other side.

Huddling against the side of an old grey-stone, I managed to
inch my way into its doorway. It looked as if no one had entered
there in a very long time. Perhaps it was an abandoned shop. I
was hoping the rain would slow and the fog would move away,
for it was turning cold. Holly huddled close to me, her black fur
drenched and smelly. I patted her head, her pitiful brown eyes all
a wonder. "We'll soon find home, girl."

She shuddered. "So, you doubt me?" Just then a man hurried past. It was Mr Cooke, from his lordship's Great House.
"Sir!" I shouted and bolted from the doorway after him. "Sir,
please, if I may ..."

Holding his black umbrella, he slowed and glanced around,
I knew he didn't see me.

"Down here, sir!" I tugged at his waistcoat.

Still looking around, he continued to hurry along. I ran
alongside. "Sir," I tugged harder, "I cannot find home." Holly was
at my heels.

He stopped and looked down at me. "Home?"

Wiping my face, I nodded. "For leaving the Great House
from a different way, I got lost, sir."

"Well, what do you want me to do about it? I have no idea
where you live. That is, if you really live in a house."

I thought of our ramshackle place in the alley. "Oh, I assure
you, sir, I do."

He looked me up and down. He looked at Holly and shook
his head. "I can't be bothered with the likes of your kind." He
shook his umbrella at us and hurried away. I watched him move
up the street, and just as he was to turn the corner, he slipped.
The package he was carrying scattered along the walk. People
coming and going stepped around him, frowning. I overheard
them cursing him as being a drunkard.

"Oh, he isn't drinking," I corrected as I picked up the things
strewn along the walk. His hat had toppled into the gutter and
swirled its way down the street. His umbrella, caught by the alleyway wind, flew up and into the fog. "Oh, sir," Holly and I hurried to his side. "Are you hurt?"

"Do I look like I'm hurt?" he said with a sour expression.

"No."

"Then help me to my feet."

Holly and I helped him up. By now he was drenched, his
once finely combed black hair hung about his shoulders, drip-

ping.

"Oh, where's my hat, my umbrella, my ...?"

"I'll get your hat, sir, but your umbrella flew away." I pointed toward the soggy dung pile the street sweeps had shovelled aside. Hurrying back with his hat, I handed it to him.

Snatching it from my hand, he shook his head in disgust. "I worked for a solid month to pay for this silk beauty!"

I nodded. "It is a beautiful hat, sir."

"Once a beautiful hat!"

Holly and I stared at it. I nodded. "I happened to pick up these things that fell out of your package, sir."

"What?" He rubbed the rain from his eyes. "What things?"

I held up two wrapped articles. "That package you were carrying when you fell. I picked them up. If there were more, I don't know what happened to them, sir."

He grabbed the articles from my grasp and looked them over. "Come out of the rain, Pauper, is it?"

"Poppy, sir." I followed him into Bakewell's Bakery and was met with glares.

Cooke growled at the owner. "She's with me, so be about your business."

The shop-keeper frowned at me. "Very well, sir." Within a minute he had returned and took Cooke's order of tea and tarts—berry tarts, warm with butter.

"I suppose I should say thank you for helping me out there, miss. Nasty weather this day, that's for sure."

"Oh, you are very welcome, sir." Holly sat by my side, half-hidden by Mr Cooke, trembling from the cold I imagine or from his gruff voice.

He patted his black silk hat on an old hearth grate and then gently lay it on the chair. Brushing rain from his shoulders, he frowned at me. "So, you're lost?"

I was beginning to shiver, I had no shawl, no bonnet, and my shoes were soggy. "I have never been lost before, sir. And I do not know how I should have done such a thing, but I do know Mama is probably searching for me." I glanced out the window, it was now early evening. The lit candle on our table flickered into the window. "I must soon be going, sir. Mama will be in a fright."

"Now how can you do such a thing when you don't even know where you're going?"

I shrugged. "We'll just keep searching, I suppose, sir."

"What's the name of the street where you live?"

"Ah, we live in an alley, it has no name."

"Well, it can't be far from here."

I nodded in doubt. "But, I don't know where *here* is, sir."

"You know where the river is, don't you?"

"Yes."

"Well," he pointed, "it is just there, by a few blocks."

I thought for a moment. "But for the fog, I cannot reason exactly how to find my way."

Our tea and tarts were set before us. When Mr Cooke turned to his tea, the waiter held his nose at me.

"I don't suppose you know how to pour," eyeing me in doubt.

"Well, I know how to drink."

Guffawing loudly, he shook his head and poured a goodly portion into my cup. "Here, you probably know how to eat these tarts, then."

I gladly took the tart, and when Cooke glanced away, I gave half my portion to Holly. "Thank you, sir."

"Have another."

Glancing out the window, I saw Mama walk past. I jumped up and dashed out the door. "Mama! Mama!"

She turned and hurried back to me, her face shiny with rain; her headscarf soaked and droopy. "Grace, where have you been? I have been walking up and down the streets searching for you."

"Oh, I know Mama. I got lost."

She looked at me in doubt. "Lost? Why, how can that be?"

"Madam," said Cooke, "I assure you, Miss Pauper was led in the wrong direction from Lord Allenton's Great House. I insisted she leave by the front entrance, rather than from the garden. It became foggy, it began to rain, and I am assuming she became disoriented. You mustn't be too harsh. And, I might add, she saved my life."

Mama's jaw dropped, she stammered, "Why, I ... had no idea, sir."

"Come in from the rain, madam. Pauper and I were just sitting down for a little cup of tea and tarts. Do join us."

Mama followed us back into the bakery. After removing her tattered shawl and soaked gloves, she nervously sat. "Jumping up and much agitated, she glanced back at her seat. "Oh, beg pardon, sir." Taking up Cooke's squashed hat, she turned paler. "Oh, sir, I ..."

With what appeared to be a great amount of distress, he reached for his hat. With his fist, he punched out the creases, tapped it again on the grate and sat it under his chair. I might add, where I had thought all along it should have been placed.

He read my mind.

Without further mention of the unfortunate occurrence, Cooke stood. Holly remained under the table, curled up very near the hearth fire. "Allow me, madam, to take your umbrella." He glanced down. "It is pooling on the floor."

Mama pushed back from the table. "Oh, indeed, sir, thank you. I might have slipped, how kind of you to notice."

Examining Mama's umbrella, full of holes, with a shake of his head, he hung it on the stand. "Allow me to introduce myself, madam. My name is Mr Francis Cooke, Lord Allenton's butler."

Mama nodded, her bottom lip quivered. She was probably too scared to even speak. I handed her my half cup of tea. "Here, Mama, it is still warm."

Her hands were trembling when she took the cup, but she managed to bring it to her lips without spilling a drop."

"Indeed, have a warm berry tart, madam."

"Oh, thank you, sir." Mama reached out and with her red and swollen hands took one." Smiling at Mr Cooke, she deftly bit into it.

"So, you mend books, do you?"

I sat up proudly. "And I read them, sir."

Mama nodded. Swallowing, she finished off the tea. "I also sew, do cobbler work, take in laundry ... very many things, sir."

Cooke nodded. "Ah, yes, clean shoes. I did not know who her ladyship sent her shoes to, but so she does."

I was thankful he didn't mention how Mama forgot to flatten her ladyship's heels.

"Grace saved your life, sir?" she asked dabbing a trickle of rain from her forehead.

Cooke cocked his ear as if to make certain her words. "Grace?" He looked down at me. "You said your name was Pauper."

"Poppy, sir."

"I detest the nickname, Mr Cooke," said Mama with a frown. But the men find it charming and tip her extra."

"I see," said Cooke. "Well, all the same, I slipped in the rain, and she came to my aid ... helped me up, so she did."

I nodded. "And I found your hat and those two packages, sir." I reminded him.

"Oh, yes," he glanced down at his hat, still dented, but firm, though soaked through and shiny, heavy with rain. Patting his vest pocket, he smiled. "She recovered my ring, been in the family for many years." He nodded. "I suppose the other things matter little."

Mama smiled at me. "She's a good one, Mr Cooke." She finished her tea and stood. "We must return home. It is late, sir, and we have much to do."

"I know, Mama, I suppose we'll be the night ironing."

Cooke helped Mama with her coat. "Where is your husband, madam?"

I looked up at him. "We don't have one, sir. He sailed away a long time ago, even before I was ..."

"Grace," said Mama as she kicked my foot, "Mr Cooke was just being polite." She put her damp scarf about her head with a shiver. "Good evening, sir. Thank you for the tea and sweets."

Cooke walked up to the door and glanced out. "It is foggy and cold." He took his waistcoat off and put it over my shoulders. "Allow me to see you home. This neighbourhood is rife with scoundrels anymore." He withdrew from his pocket a few coins and tossed them atop the table. "Come, then, shall we?"

Holly scurried from under the table and stood at my side as Cooke retrieved his hat. Placing it on his head, we left the bakery. His coat felt very warm and dry.

"Thank you, sir." I noticed the sleeves nearly scraped the street. My skinny little arms hung limp inside, but warm.

All the way home Cooke talked about this and that, Mama nodded. I was in amazed wonder when we reached our alley. How could I have missed travelling up but one lane and then turning down another?

Mama used her most proper words, and put on her most proper face. "Thank you Mr Cooke, Grace and I shall ever be in your debt. When next you need a favour sir, you know where we can be found."

"Indeed, Mrs Pauper. Good evening."

Mama and I entered our little shelter of a house. Hanging about every hook was the laundry. "Hurry them down, Grace. They are good for ironing, moist and all."

"Yes, Mama."

We finished everything by the time the town clock struck midnight. Holly was asleep at the hearth though barely a glow on the grate. Each laundry bundle was wrapped and pinned. I knew by the colour how that Mama tied who the wash belonged to.

"In the morning, Grace, you will take them out, but for now it is late, and you must go to bed."

I nodded and slipped out of my wet shoes and hung my woollen socks on the fire screen. Removing my apron, I hung it on a peg. Hearing a clinking noise, I spied a silvery flash roll about the floor. Picking it up, I studied its patina under light from a hanging candle. "Mama, it is Mr Cooke's ring." Turning around I found that she had left the room. When I went to find her, she was already asleep. I held the ring secure in my hand wondering where I could have found such an item and concluded it somehow found its way into my apron pocket when Cooke put his coat about my shoulders. I thought for a second about hurrying away into the night to return it to him, it was his family's. Standing at the open door, it was now raining very hard. "I shall return it to him in the morning."

Climbing into bed, I snuggled close to Mama. Her sharp little bones were stretched thin, but warm. Her breathing was soft and narrow. "I love you Mama." I clutched the ring and fell off to sleep.

*** * ***

"Grace, hurry along now and waken."

Sitting up, I found the room as I left it and hoped the sun was shining. I remembered the ring, but during the night it had slipped from my hands. Burrowing beneath the covers, I retrieved it. At the window, I found it even more beautiful than under candlelight. It was a silver filigree ring. All around it icy glittery little stars sparkled, and in its centre a very beautiful, clear white stone, sparkling in the light of day.

"Hurry along Grace. I will sweep the corner and then be on to the lending library. Meet me there at seven. Eat first and then deliver the bundles."

I heard the door latch before I could even drop my legs over the bed. "Yes, Mama." I hurried from bed, and found my stockings now dry. Slipping my feet into my shoes, they still felt damp and cold. Finishing dressing I tied my apron into a neat bow. I had to look neat, or else no one would believe me.

I slipped the ring back into my apron pocket. After delivering the bundles to The Red Teapot, Hanny's Silver Shop, and the Mistress Flannigan, I hurried down the alley to Lord Allenton's in search of Mr Cooke. I did not bring Holly along, I simply did not have time to keep her at my side.

I reached the white gate to his lordship's garden and hesitated. Perhaps I should go around the front this time. I know I provoked Cooke, he did not believe me when I said the gate was unlocked. This time I tried the gate, indeed it was locked, but such a silly thing to do, why, anyone with one leg could surely hop over such a small fence.

Hurrying out front, I noticed the walks had not been swept. His lordship would not be inclined to favour such a thing. Mrs Morgan's broom (she's the housekeeper) was propped up next to the spring flowering pots, and I had the notion to at least clear away the leaves nestled about the carriage-porch steps lest they find their way into the house.

Glancing around, I found the street to be teeming with coaches, wagons, and street sweepers. I noticed Mama's friend, Mrs Shanihan at her corner sweeping, she was favoured by her ladyship for she kept the walks and places she travelled clean so that her hems would not likely become soiled. Mama hated washing and sewing raggedy filthy hems, but *beggars should not be choosers.* [1]

Now done with sweeping the carriage-porch, I went up to the door, and still not tall enough to reach the bell-pull, I took the broom handle and pushed at the yawning-faced-lion brass knocker. Clang clang clang, such a disturbing racket to be sure, but still no one came. As I tried the knob, the door swung open, easily and without even a creak. Stepping inside, I sniffed the dark, dank air finding a sour repose of neglected fire pits. The sun was at my back now, and it lent a shiny glow about the room. Here I found the wall sconces clear, tapers full and unused. The floors were clean, an eerie disquietude tapped my brow – the quietness about this great mansion seemed out of place.

I removed the ring from the apron pocket and held it to the sun's light. It sparkled red, blue, green—the colours of a brilliant rainbow. The silver gleamed, a patina of great magnitude, I supposed. Suddenly the wind picked up and slammed the door violently behind me.

"Who's there?" Came a gruff voice.

I backed up. The hair on my neck bristled, I answered the faceless voice. "Me, sir, I have come to see Cooke."

A huge fellow came from around his lordship's study door. "Cook has gone on to his lordship's country home. Now, how the devil did you let yourself in?"

---

1. English proverb. First recorded by John Heywood (1497-1580) English playwright. Quoted from *The Proverbs, Epigrams, and Miscellanies of John Heywood* (1906), p 170. "Beggars should be no choosers: but yet they will;"

"I couldn't reach the bell, sir, so I pushed at the lion's big mouth."

"Couldn't reach the bell, indeed!" He looked me up and down. "Pushed at the lion's big mouth? What sort of excuse is that, I should like to know, to let one's self in? Such a nerve." He tugged rudely on my braid. "I should call the constable and have you taken to the poor house by the looks of you."

"I am sorry, sir. I simply had come to see Cooke, and nothing more."

"And nothing more? Who do you suppose lives here? I want you to answer that one."

"Lord Allenton, I sell him daisies."

"Now I know you're up to mischief. Why, daisies are a least two months from sprouting."

"Oh, indeed, sir, I know that as well. I meant only that when they push up from the earth, my mother gathers them and wraps them tied with a nice piece of string and I ..."

"Enough of your claptrap, go away. I'm much too busy for your gibberish."

I felt the ring in my apron pocket and decided I must try another way to find Mr Cooke. A strange feeling settled about my shoulders as I sighed deeply. "Well, then, sir, I will be going."

"The name's Buffle, Mr Buffle to you." He pointed with a grunt. "And there's the door." He frowned. "Wait just a minute," he said moving to the door and examining the latch in great detail. "It was locked." He peered down into my face. "Don't tell me, little girl, that you found it open."

I nodded. "Just like the garden gate, sir."

"What?"

"Yesterday I came to deliver her ladyship's shoes and came in from the alley. And the gate was open as well as the servants' door."

The portly gentleman looked puzzled. "That cannot be, little girl. I locked every gate, every window, and every door myself."

"Not every one, sir."

Scratching his head, I could tell he was not quite certain that he could even remember his name.

"Is that so? Well, then, where is her ladyship's shoes if you are telling the truth, which I doubt."

"I gave them to Cooke yesterday."

He glanced at the ceiling. "Look about the room, will you. Do you see any shoes? Do you see this cook?"

"No sir, but I was told by him that her ladyship's heels would render them useless ... she would wobble about so."

He felt my brow, shaking his head. "I'll not listen to another absurdity. Where are your mother and father, I should like to know?"

"I do not have a father, Mr Buffle. My mother is waiting for me at the lending library." I headed for the door. "I am late, sir, and must be going."

"What is your name, little girl?"

"Poppy, sir."

"Well, Poppy, from now on I would not be so bold as to walk into someone's home without first knocking."

"Yes, sir." I opened the door and turned back. "Will his lordship return soon, sir?"

"That is none of your concern, miss."

I closed the door quietly behind me, feeling his glare burrowing into the back of my head. I quickly descended the porch steps. Once out and on the walk, I hurriedly skipped up the alley. Passing his lordship's cellar window, I stopped. The window was broken. Shards of thick, wavy glass were lying about. Peeking in, I could see lumps of coal and dust and old dried flowers hanging from line hooks from the ceiling. Water had drained into the room from last night's rain. I thought about going back and telling Mr Buffle of my discovery, but I knew Mama was waiting for me at the library and hurried away.

I will come back tomorrow. I know his lordship's Great House was in need of repair and sweeping. He would be mighty upset to return home and find such a messy garden, messy carriage-porch, messy this and that.

* * *

"Grace," said Mama in a cross tone, "where have you been?"

I pulled out the ring and showed it to her. "You were asleep last night else I would have shown it to you, Mama. This morning after delivering the bundles, I went back to Lord Allenton's to find Mr Cooke and return his ring."

"Well, now," she studied the ring with fascination, "this is a beauty, Grace." She looked at me. "Yes, I remember Mr Cooke patting his vest pocket smiling that he had his family's ring safe and sound." She smiled at me and patted my head. "He was not there, Grace?"

"No, Mama, just a plump, grumbling old sort of fellow, Mr

Buffle." Rather exasperated, I shook my head. "He said Mr Cooke has gone on to his lordship's country home."

Mama looked disappointed. Still examining the ring, her brows furrowed. "Do you know where his lordship's country estate is, Grace? I do not think it wise to hand this over to just anyone."

I nodded. "Indeed, Mama. Mr Cooke must be frantic at such a loss. Do you suppose when he put his coat over me last night the ring somehow found its way into my apron pocket?"

"How else, Grace?" She nodded with a smile. "And such a stroke of good luck for him. I am sure he will be pleased with its return, perhaps a small reward even."

"But, Mama, how are we to find his lordship's estate? It is well over twenty miles, a great distance."

"Oh, not such a great walking distance, Grace. We could do it in a long day, surely." She put the ring in a jar on the mantle ledge. "Now, take these books. We have much to do to repair them. I must have them done by tomorrow morning when the lending library opens, or they won't pay me." She frowned, peering down into my apron pocket. "And, you didn't get a penny for Lady Allenton's shoes?"

"No, Mama, I was about to tell you that Mr Cooke said the work wasn't worth a penny."

Shaking her head, she was clearly irritated with me. "Hurry along, then, Grace. We have a lot of books to mend."

Chapter 2 – Poppy Sent to Prison

The following morning I awoke with Holly licking my face. Giggling, I set her aside. "You must jump down, girl. I have much to do today. I will sweep Lord Allenton's porch and ..." I sat up rubbing my eyes "... and while there I will visit the mews, perhaps one of the stable boys knows where his lordship's country house is."

Jumping from bed, I glanced up at the jar that held the ring. "I will take it with me just in case Mr Cooke has returned."

Hurrying out the door, I spied Holly peering out the window, whining. "Oh, dear girl, you may come along next time. I'm trying to find the whereabouts of his lordship's country house." I took the ring out of my apron pocket and showed it to her through the window. "You see, Mama and I must return this ring to its proper owner." I blew her kisses. "Good-bye girl." I skipped along the slop strewn alleyway until finally coming to his lordship's garden. The gate was locked, and the only way to the mews was to climb over the fence. I patted my apron pocket and felt the ring safe and secure.

Looking around, I did not see anyone and continued my way through the tall damp grass to the carriage-house. Pushing open the tall, wide wooden door, I crept in. It was dark and dank, the hard-packed dirt floor was dry and dusty, deep runnels of hoof marks ran up and down the passage-way inside. Walking about, one of the horses nickered, a fine bay, silky and well-mannered. I petted its soft muzzle and glanced into his stall, someone had just been here for its manger was full of hay. Sweet, yellow straw lay scattered at its feet. As he hung his head over the half-door, he sniffed my hair. Giggling, I kissed his soft, prickly muzzle. He nickered. "You're a fine fellow."

Glancing around I found pitchforks and black wrought iron hooks hanging from the wall. Sniffing the air, I found the sweet smell of hay to be quite different than the horses' manure, though both made my nose itch. Ambling around I found a staircase—perhaps where I might find a friendly servant sympathetic to one of his own.

Climbing the stairs, I swept away cobwebs, suspicious of lurking spiders hidden inside tiny dark spiral holes of dust. Shaking my head in disgust, someone's not been here in a very long time. Why, any groom worth his salt would not have a web anywhere within the tip of his broom. Now standing at the top of the staircase, I froze. There came a tap, tap, tap. Following the noise, I came to a door and leaned my ear to it, listening. I heard the tap again and tried the door, but it would not open.

Now knocking lightly, I listened for a beckon, but only came the same odd tapping. *Hmm, where might a key be hidden?* I ran my hand along the roughhewn door ledge but, ouch, I found only splinters.

I gingerly put my ear to the door again and called, "Mr Cooke? Is that you?" Hearing a mumble in return, I knew exactly that this was no trapped bird or the scamper of a mouse. I must soon find out for myself.

Searching about the long-shaped hall for a dangle of keys, I found none. Suddenly I heard the stable door below open and slam shut. I ran to the end of the room and hid behind some old wooden yokes and harness gear. I did not want to be found again. I patted my apron pocket, the ring was secure.

I held my breath as I heard the heavy footfalls ascend the steps, shortly a dark figure of a man made his way directly to the locked door. He passed by the one lone window, and I noticed the dull yellow silver of his hair hanging about his shoulders. His waistcoat was short-sleeved, his trousers too short for his blackened, mud-caked boots. He held a large package and settled it at his feet as he withdrew from his pocket a key. With clumsy abandon, he noisily inserted it into the lock. Now kicking the door open, he shuffled in. My heart beat so loud I was sure he could hear it, when suddenly I heard his voice. He was arguing, but with whom I was not at all sure.

The tapping came about again. I pondered the thought of easing up to the door. When I stood, I heard the door creak open again, and I leaned back, hoping he wouldn't look my way.

He reached out and grabbed the package he had left on the floor at the door's entrance. I heard him rattle it about, I imagined food. Was he feeding a monster? Within a little time, he left the room, not locking it behind him. He was to soon return or perhaps he just forgot.

When he was long out of sight, I tiptoed to the top of the staircase. He left through the stable door at last. He was no stable boy that was for sure. Tiptoeing back to the door, I held my breath and peeked in. I gaped. "Your lordship!"

There sitting on a rickety old chair was Lord Allenton, his eyes bulging at me, a pitiful stare if there ever was one. His wrists and legs secured by leather harnesses; his mouth secured with a rag; his once immaculately kept hair now rumpled.

"Oh, dear me, sir!" Just then I heard the door down below open and the rustle of someone entering. Frantically glancing around, the room was spare, not a thing to hide behind, but his lordship for one. I thanked God he was of a portly nature, I squatted behind him. Tucking my skirt beneath, I hugged the back of his chair and holding my breath, I kept my eyes closed.

The door opened. I thanked my lucky stars the room was dark, for the window was golden dim with dust, thick and plentiful, stuck to the panes.

"Here, you fat one, drink this." The man's voice was raspy and ignorant. As he untied the rag from about his lordship's mouth, he grunted, "Be quick, I ain't got all day with the likes of you."

His lordship pleaded for a sip of water, but instead, the coarse man poured something down his throat. I think it was gin, because it dripped into my hair. His lordship spit up. I heard a gag, a moan, and then nothing.

"Very well, then, spit it all away, you old fool, but that's what you're getting for a day's portion."

With that the man retied the rag around his lordship's head and left, pulling the door closed behind him. Standing up, I whispered to his lordship. "Sir, I will untie you." I took the rag from his mouth.

"Oh, who are you?" His eyes were squinty and watery, his speech slurry. He nervously glanced about. "Be ever so quiet, they are near about, I would wager."

I remained huddled about him as I tried to untie his hands. "The straps are very tight, sir."

"Oh, be very quiet, are you a little girl?"

He tried to move his wrists, but they were bruised and I thought them to be sore. I nodded. "Yes, I am Poppy. You probably don't remember me, sir."

"Oh, my legs are sore. I can barely feel them," he whispered with a moan.

I finally got his hands and legs loose. I noticed a thankful smile on his lips, though terribly chapped. "Dreadful, your lordship. Do ye know these bad men, sir?"

"Yes, I ..."

"Oh, just one moment, sir, I am almost finished, sir."

"Oh, child, how can I thank you? You are very brave."

Now I had finished with untying his legs, and he stood slowly, holding his back, rubbing his thighs. "Stay here, sir. I will see if he is gone."

I tip-toed quiet as a cat over the floor and to the door and opened it. "They are gone, sir. Come, we shall escape."

His lordship could barely walk. Teetering, I offered him my shoulder. "There you go, sir. You may lean on me." I smelled gin on his breath. "Are you drunk, sir?" I felt him stiffen. "I beg your pardon, sir. It is just that ..."

"They've been pouring gin down my throat for a very long time."

"Oh, why would they do such a thing, sir?"

"Money, jewels," he shrugged, "I wish I knew, little girl." We heard a noise, and he pointed to the back of the barn. "That way."

"My name's Poppy, sir." I held tight to his hand as we quietly hurried to the back of the room, where to my surprise was a dark and narrow passage down into the stables below. "They'll not find us here, sir."

"Oh, they are very clever. Once outside you must run like the very wind and go to the police."

"We must run together, sir, I would not want to leave you."

"Oh, I shall remain hidden, until you come back. I am an old man, half-drunk my dear, and cannot run."

"Well, I shall not leave you behind. We shall go together."

He fondly tugged one of my braids. "Very well, then, Poppy."

We tiptoed down the very narrow stairs, it was very dark and dusty—cobwebs hung everywhere. "I will kill every one of them, sir. Depend upon it."

"But you are too little, my dear."

"Not so, sir, I kill them at every notice."

"Thieves?" He whispered in amazement.

"Spiders, sir, I hate them. They have far too many eyes to suit me." Nearing the bottom, I glanced around to the nickering of the horses. "They are watching me, sir."

His lordship froze. "Spiders?"

"Your carriage horses, sir, the scrounger is nowhere to be found. Come then, sir." I was about to hurry out through the stable doors in the front when his lordship tugged on my apron. "No," he whispered, "this way."

I followed him through another small space where we had

to crouch low through a tunnel of sorts and then I saw daylight through a small door just ahead.

"I'll go first, little girl, just in case they are lurking."

He slowly crawled out from the side of the stables that led into his apple orchard. There were raspberry bushes, blackberry bushes, all sorts of prickly little obstructions, but that did not deter either of us. We crawled along the side until we were well hidden by his carriage equipage and very much scratched by the prickly bushes, my hands were full of thorns, my hair with twigs and leaves of all sorts.

Now standing, we brushed ourselves off, for who would believe poor Lord Allenton was really a lord. His waistcoat was filthy with dust, his shirt cuffs brown and torn, his trousers mightily creased from the harness. Down the front of his once immaculate white ruffled shirt were stains, chunks of wormy foodstuffs held fast to his buttonholes.

"Stay right there!" said a voice just behind us.

Turning I found a policeman. "Oh, glory be." I sighed in relief, thankful for such a miraculous find.

His lordship straightened. A dignified drawl escaped his red, cracked, and chapped lips. His speech slurred, "Oh, my good man, why my little friend and I were just on our way to find you." He teetered on his feet, and I steadied him.

"Is that so?" The policeman looked him up and down with disbelief. "And who might you be?"

"Lord Allenton." He gestured with his shaky white, scaly finger toward the Great House. "And that is where I live, I'll have you know."

Looking down his red, bulbous nose, the policeman nodded with an air of disbelief and withdrew his baton.

"Indeed it is, sir," I said wiping cobwebs from my face, feeling as if a crawly sort of intruder was scrambling down my back, I fidgeted. The policeman held a doubtful glare, not at all convinced, due to the fact, I am very sure, of our appearance.

"Indeed," his wooden baton tapped his leg, "and what business do you have here, imp?" he said, eyeing me with the same suspicion as he had to his lordship.

"I have come to return this ring." I pulled it from my apron pocket and held it out for him to examine the truthfulness of my confession.

Suddenly his lordship gasped. Wiping his eyes, he cried, "Why, that ring belonged to my wife, it was stolen some time ago." He searched my face. "How did you come upon it, little girl?"

When he reached for it, O'Malacy kicked him. "Stay put, thief." The constable grabbed the ring, examined it briefly, snorted, and stuffed it into his holding purse. Grabbing one of my braids, he then took the back of his lordship's collar and pushed him right ahead. "Well, well, now we know who to blame, don't we, little girl. He glanced at Lord Allenton with a sneer.

"Do not handle me thus," said his lordship as he tried to free himself. "Do you have any idea who I am?"

"I know who you are, but nobody else will." With a rude push, he growled, "Now move along before I box your ears—aye, now dirty enough to grow potatoes, you old fool."

I knew within my heart I would never see mama or his lordship ever again. We were marched to the police station like common thieves. Just before entering the red brick building, I glanced back and found Mr Buffle standing at a distance staring after us. Wiggling to be free, I shouted, "Oh, Mr Buffle, for mercy, vouch for us."

The policeman wrapped my braid around his thick wrist and pulled me up the steps with such a force. "Enough, imp." He looked back at Buffle. "Know him do you?"

Feeling pain from his grip, I nodded, trying to free myself. "You must let me go."

"Jewellery thief, I will not."

"Mr Buffle," I shouted back at him, "please help us."

"That man is not Buffle, so hold your tongue before I pluck it out altogether."

Chapter 3 – Twelve Years Hence – The Search for Mother

Twelve years have passed since I was falsely thrown into prison in Brighton, and now set free, I sit staring out at the British sea—the glimmer of wet leaves set upon the drifts of waves, black and mouldy as if set before me as a reminder of my past. Indeed, I sat wondering where I might begin my new life. Twenty and two, and at last breathing the light of a fresh day I wondered only what this new life would bring, or what could I bring to it. I thought again of Mama and what might have become of her. How frantic she must have been searching for me, but her only child, Grace Wilson, no longer existed, and for whatever reason, the policeman, O'Malacy, who arrested Lord Allenton and me, gave me the name Anne Philips. Why would someone want to take away my name?

My home these past months was at the edge of the woods where I found a hollow tree and soft dry leaves to set my head. To build a fire was of no great work. As a rag and bone girl, I found many usable wares in which to eat and drink. The stars at night were my visions of a happier place, far beyond the uncertainty of city people.

Someday I would work my way from the prison life I had grown to remember. I had made friends with a few of the girls my own age while there, but they did not understand my thinking, my agility of numbers, and the proper order of things. People somehow became confused and distrustful of me.

Indeed, my words confounded almost everyone in the little circle of humans that surrounded my sphere of breathing. In prison, I learned to sing rather than converse in meaningless chatter. And along the way, I would mimic the little brown birds that made their nests within the walls of the holding pen of a waste-land—an island for desperate people of no wealth, but of a hearty will of life. I was thankful, because I heard some prisoners were sent to America or Australia, and even the children who were not supposed to be there, were sent away. I know.

Most of my acquaintances had been caught stealing bread, sometimes just a snatch not fit for a bird. Mary Agnes Bennett, my friend, was sent to prison because one night in a gin house she sipped from a dusty, half-empty bottle sitting in a nook. She didn't know it was shelved there for a wealthy sea merchant upon his return. Being rudely pushed into the wall by the proprietor, she aptly spit in his face.

I remember very well her words: 'Well, I'd do it again, Poppy, mind my word.' She slapped her thigh. 'He broke me nose, and when I've finished my time here, I'm goin' back to that gin house.' " She coughed violently into the dank air. 'And this time I'll spit in his soup when 'es fat arse is pointin' at me face.'

'Tis what I'd do, Mrs Bennett.' I patted her back. 'He had no right in shoving you like that.' I studied her crooked nose. 'He had no right, and I am sorry for you.'

She took my hand. "I knowed you are, Poppy. With all your fancy words, and a whistlin' to the birds, you bring somethin' into these walls. You settle us with your peaceful ways, even makin' friends with them scurry ol' rats."

Ah, if I could only speak aloud the anger and hurt that that lingers in my heart as easily, but for me, it seems, I can only speak aloud to the soft wind, convinced I had to or my voice would surely dry up into dust. I envisioned my words meandering up and all about the errant air spent and lifeless, but I was not so lifeless as to give up finding my dearest Mama. I will find her. Being released from prison in Brighton, a hundred miles north by any means to London, was a very distant sum of footfalls. And I wasn't at all certain in which direction to first set-off.

"Excuse me, miss," came a soft-spoken voice, from behind. "I am looking for a certain Melville Lane. Might you be familiar with it?"

Turning to his words, I shook my head. By then he had noticed my soiled, grey prison apron, the tattered scarf, the rancid tone of my cheek. He touched his hat. "Beg pardon." He swiftly walked away holding a handkerchief to his nose.

Glancing down at the dry grass and rubbish all about me, I sighed deeply. "I must soon find suitable clothes. Even a scullery maid dressed better." Remembering that we used to hang our clothes to dry in the alley, I glanced around, perhaps wandering a little ways into a dark passage I might find a discarded rag or two.

Rummaging through the trash bins, I was lucky enough to find a broom. Though broken and half loose of its straw it would do well at any street corner. I knew how to mend such a broom. And if I did good work sweeping, a handsome tip would surely follow. I couldn't just assume any portion of a street, for most street sweepers had set their claim. I finally assumed an abandoned corner and kept a neat track, well-tended from any sort of rubbish, dung, broken carriage wheels, thrown horseshoes ... indeed, I was earnest and hardworking for the upper classes that chose my corner to cross.

Gentlemen in open carriages would toss me coins for my work. I made friends with Mr Sharp, Luck's Flower Shop, for sweeping his step freely. In exchange, he gave me day-old flowers to sell for myself.

Now becoming a little sleepy, I watched the crescent moon dip out a spot on the black night above my eyes. The thought of my prison people visited me often, and how Mary Agnes would put us little ones in the corner and sleep atop us, for the guards were always eyeing the littlest of maidens. One swift kick in the smallest part of a man's trousers sent them on their way. I will always cherish the memory and spirit of Mary Agnes. Indeed, I must always cherish how well I live today while just yesterday, mere hours distant, bleak prison walls.

Rain woke me. Scooting farther beneath the old oak tree that grew near the river's edge, I watched a cluster of tiny brown birds sipping droplets of water trapped on a leaf. I watched them for a little while, afraid if I sat up I would frighten them away, but they soon drank enough and flew off. I spied some lovely wildflowers just beyond the water's edge. After breakfast, I will gather a bunch and sell them in the village. I reached for my purse and counted my money—always at first light, even before I made my fire. Within the month I would have saved enough to travel to London. I had bought proper boots, planning on such a trek in advance. My clothes were fit to stop along the way and do servant's work.

I hid my little roll of belongings under a bush, took my broken broom and left my little place well hidden under the mantle of the old oak.

Wherever I go, I study the faces all around me. Perhaps I will find an old friend. When I search through the rubbish piles, I smile at those digging alongside me as I seek a familiarity. Could any one of them be my prison family?

Someday I would earn enough money to set off on my own to find Mama. By now, Holly must have died, for she would visit me in my dreams betimes, deliriously happy to find me, but for a few seconds. And then she would run off in a misty whirl of black fur—always a happy reunion with a bid of returning again someday.

I knew how to curtsey, knew how to act proper; knew how to read. Should anyone ask, I had my reasons for travelling well sorted out. Prison was a forbidden topic. I knew that very well. Besides, I was not a thief. Someday when I am in an affable situation in life, I will confess my twelve years of imprisonment after finding Mama, his lordship, and Mr Cooke, that is. They were my only hope of grace. I worried they were dead, along with Holly.

Now and again I'd stop at a trough and question a footman or groomsman about the way to London, and if they had ever heard of a Lord Allenton, but I was met with sneers and snubs. What right had a beggar to ask such questions? Did they smell the prison stench upon my hair, my breath? I bathed in the warmest part of day, and bought clothes that a respectable maid might wear. But alas, my hands, perhaps, gave me away. I must remember to wear gloves.

I did find the London Road and worked my way along it, careful to hide at the proper notice. Being alone had its good tidings, but more often than not, it was dangerous for a woman alone. Highwaymen rode up and down searching, always searching.

I learned that the London Road ran north then east, for the most part, and ran crooked as a ribbon sometimes. I also learned the sun came up in the east and set in the west. Now standing in the middle of the road, it was baked solid, beige and hot. To my right, the wheat fields were awash in golden honey light. At the moment, the sun was directly atop my head.

I often sheltered in the heat of the day, and watched the shadows as they moved short then long. Watched the sun set, and knew in which direction to keep moving. I kept my ear cocked for riders and stagecoaches as they cared not for pedestrians making way along *their* road, and as likely as not, would trample us without a moment's pause.

Coming upon the tip of a hill I noticed a fingerpost pointing down into a small village at the bottom of a twisty path. *Peabury?* Why, I had often heard Mama mention such a place when she'd read to me, but that was so long ago. I followed the twisty little path down and hoped the air would be cooler there. A small stream meandered alongside the path. Far up and to my right grazed a cow with her newborn. Passing a few cottages, I stopped to admire the lovely flower gardens, primroses, the thorny blackberry, and the leafy green potato shrubs. While admiring one particular garden, a woman stepped from her door. "You're a new one to Crawley, are you?"

"Oh, yes, ma'am. I'm on my way to London." I turned and pointed up from where I had descended, "and noticed your lovely village thinking it was cooler here."

The cottager nodded. "Tis a nice one." She stood staring at me, examining my clothes. I noticed the twitch of her nose.

I smiled. "Indeed, ma'am, I'm in search of my mother. She lived in London last we spoke."

"Ah, yes we get separated betimes, but 'tis good you're lookin' for her."

I nodded. "Yes, I'll be on my way then, it's a rather long walk. About another ..."

"Forty, by the road," she said, "but, you can take the path you're on." She pushed open the gate and came out to point the way. "Continue on this path to the stream, follow it down a-ways and it will take you back to the London road. Saves a mile or two," she smiled, her one eye seemed to float from my hair to my mouth.

"Why, thank you. My name is Miss Grace Wilson."

"Mauve Milbrew, my husband's in the field. You'll pass him soon enough."

I wished the pleasant cottager a good afternoon and moved up the path and then stopped and turned back to her. "Mrs Milbrew, might you be familiar with the name Allenton?"

Her face puckered in the sun as she thought. "No, but you might ask along the way."

I nodded and moved on. "Indeed, thank you."

"Say, miss, might you be interested in a little work?"

"What type of work?"

"There is to be a grand celebration at Peabury, the Great House, just yonder. Lord Sheffield's son is gettin' married, and they need all the help they can find. It would only be for maybe a month with cleaning, cooking, and serving. He's a kind and generous master, to be sure."

I thought for a moment. It would be easy work, and I needed money, plus a place to sleep. "Well, I should like that very much."

"The Great House is just up the path. Turn up the stream another two miles, opposite the sun."

"Thank you, Mrs Milbrew. Perhaps we shall meet again someday."

"Oh, I'll be helpin' at the grand ceremony meself."

I continued down the path. Maybe someone from the Shef-field family will be familiar with Lord Allenton. My hopes for the very first time were looking brighter. As I strolled through the tree-shrouded footpath, cool and resplendent, I heard the sound of a carriage with its squeak and groan, the snort of horses, the tangle of leather and chains. Over my shoulder, I spied the equi-page as it rolled by but twenty feet to my left. I supposed it was on the lane to the Peabury. Strapped atop with little space to add something anew were trunks, bandboxes, and portmanteau fit for royalty, I supposed. The carriage was moving quickly, and I didn't get a chance to see its occupants, just the whistle click and whip snap as the groom urged the horses on with dust curling up and settling atop everything in its wake.

Luckily for me, as I had stopped to watch the coach, I glanced back only to find a fast approaching rider on my footpath. I had seconds to jump away or be trampled. I thanked my lucky stars for landing on my backside on soft grass, for just afoot lay field rocks as big as alley cats. The rider stopped and jumped from his mount.

"Miss, I do beg your pardon!"

He helped me up, glancing me up and down. I could tell he had made up his mind that I was no doubt one of Lord Sheffield's servants, perhaps returning from the village.

"Are you hurt, miss?"

I had been warned by Mary Agnes about rough young men all loose and about always searching for young maidens in dis-tress. Indeed, honey-lipped and smooth, so they were. But surely at twenty and two, I wasn't young anymore, and for my looks, I wasn't at all certain how handsome I was.

"Oh, no, sir, I am not." My bonnet had somehow become snagged on a branch. I retrieved it and quickly began retying my bow. "But thank you, sir. I am sorry to have been in your way. I did not want to cause you alarm and hope you will not mention this incident to Lord Sheffield."

"Lord Sheffield? You know him?"

I glanced down, knowing enough not to look my betters in the eye. "No, sir, I have come from the village to help with the ceremony is all. I need the work, sir, and don't want to be consid-ered an ill omen before I even begin."

The young man laughed. "Indeed, an ill omen. Well, miss, I will not mention one word of this incident, I assure you." He slapped his hat on his thigh to rid the dust.

"Oh, thank you, sir." I glanced up to look only at his stark white cravat, but met his brilliant blue eyes instead. They caught my breath. I have never looked into such beautiful eyes in my entire life. They held the colour of the ring I found in my apron pocket many years ago. A dark shadow crossed my eyes; sadness filled my heart at such a thought. I wondered if he could tell I was recently from prison.

"Are you sure you are not hurt, miss? Why that look that crossed your face has me concerned. I am Dr Patrick Moore, a physician. Here, let me help you atop my horse and allow me to deliver you to Peabury myself."

"No, sir, I could not allow such a privilege. I am grateful for the offer, doctor, but ..."

"You certainly do not sound like a mere servant. Excuse me," he looked embarrassed, "why, you must be the new governess." He looked at my clothes, and I could tell he mistook them for being a scullery maid instead of a schooled woman. "Do forgive my presumptuous opinion of your duty, miss." He ran his fingers through his thick black hair tapping his whip to his boot.

"Sir, I am not a governess. I have come only to take what work is given to me." I was becoming nervous at all this talk, he must be wondering how I could have become so educated and be willing to accept whatever job is left to be done. I knew I had to give some explanation and offered, "My mother was educated and taught me well."

"Oh, yes, of course." He put his hat back on. "Well, then, allow me to walk the rest of the way with you. Peabury is just over the next hill."

I was beginning to feel very uncomfortable. I had never been in this part of the country in my entire life, and now I had misled this gentleman into thinking I was from the village. Perhaps I am some sort of liar after all. "I am not from the village, sir."

We began walking up the hill as I tied my bow beneath my chin.

"No? Well, that makes two of us."

I nodded, well relieved to have confessed my lie.

"But I suppose we all have to have been from some village or city or someplace." He was a tall, thin man. His pace was twice that of mine, and he slowed now and again with apologies.

I wondered if he was just trying to be silly or overly kind, but I did reason him to be a physician, one who had to love humanity or something.

"So, tell me, miss, what is your name?"

I took in a great breath. *My name?* "Miss Grace Wilson, sir."

"Ah, yes, what a lovely name."

His horse picked up its pace, crossed over and slowed to my side. She had a beautiful white blaze down her muzzle and four white socks. "She's a beauty, sir. May I pet her?"

He handed the reins to me. "She loves attention, Miss Wilson."

It had been many years since I had been alone with an animal to simply pet, kiss, and pour my heart out to its inner senses. "What is her name, sir?"

"Blossom, and it looks as if she has taken to you."

"I've never owned a horse, sir, but once a beautiful dog." I thought of Holly and blinked back tears. "But that was long ago." I stroked Blossom's warm, soft muzzle. "You are a beautiful horse, girl."

She nuzzled the nape of my neck. The prickly little hairs on her nose made me giggle. I kissed her and handed the reins back to the doctor. "Thank you, sir, I love her already. She is a *great* beauty."

Blossom nodded her head with a nicker.

The doctor laughed. "I can see that she agrees with you. You have a way with animals, miss. Did I hear you say that you once had a dog?"

"A very long time ago, sir." I must have had a sad look on my face since the doctor sighed deeply along with me.

"I am sorry it was so long ago, then. It sounds like you still miss her terribly."

I nodded, afraid to add more to the conversation. I had better stop my chattering or 'gibberish' as Mama used to say, but this kind gentleman had a way of making me talk from my heart. Words came so easily. I sensed he found me to be an intelligent woman.

The only other men who found me *intelligent* were the prison guards. They left me alone if I would read their letters to them and write in return. I even helped them with deciphering the length of sentences for the inmates, once finding that Rufus misread the sentence time of Mary Hess and let her go after finding she was held three years longer than required. That was a secret I promised to keep from the warden, and in turn, Rufus made sure the other guards kept their distance from me. I was a maiden, said Mary Agnes Bennett, and was going to stay proper, leastwise at her side.

We stopped at the top of the hill. "Ah, yes, the Great Estate, Peabury."

I took in a great breath. "Why, it is magnificent, sir." *Surely, I could be put to good work there.*

"Indeed, one of the finest water scenes I have ever seen."

I stood in awe of its beauty. All around the mansion stood oaks, elms, plums and flower gardens the likes I would probably never come across again my entire life. To the right grazed many beautiful horses.

Running to the fence, I climbed atop and waved, yelling for one of them to come to me. In the bargain, I was met with yard dogs, yelping, snarling, and barking. Along with the hounds came a few horses, their curious eyes seising upon my unfamiliar face. One particularly brave stallion, white as any cloud, nickered at me as he approached, nostrils flared, shaking his head, his ears stiff ... almost pointing at me. The others remained at a distance.

"He finds you captivating, Miss Wilson."

"Oh, sir, indeed, this is paradise." I held out my hand for the stallion to sniff my hand. "Come, boy, let me pet you." I gently petted his soft nose as two large hounds of suspicious origin sniffed at my heels, their tails wagging.

"Well, Miss Wilson, I am convinced animals are of your liking."

"Indeed, sir." I climbed from the fence and squatted to meet the dogs." I sat for a moment letting them identify that I was not to harm them. They allowed me to pet them. "Oh, sir, I have missed being around them so. I cannot tell you how much I have missed seeing them, smelling the freshness of a meadow, the sun on my shoulders ..." I knew I had better stop jabbering, perhaps I had said too much already.

Dr Moore smiled at me, as if reading my troubled mind, and simply nodded. "Well, then, come along, we must be on our way. I have an appointment, and you have a certain butler to impress. Mr Buffle, a stodgy old crust, but you'll find him good enough, I would imagine. I'll introduce you personally."

"Mr Buffle, sir?"

"Yes, that's right, Miss Wilson."

We approached the side entrance to this Great House as I imagined it to be the servants' entrance.

"I'll have Blossom taken care of. If you'd just wait right here, I'll take you to Mr Buffle.

Mr Buffle, could it be the same Buffle from Lord Allenton's Great House in London? No, of course not. Why, Buffle was an old man then and would have died by now.

"This way, Miss Wilson," said the doctor. "Mr Buffle, hopefully, is in his office."

I followed him into servants' quarters and was promptly ignored by an army of ant workers hurrying from one room to another. The aroma of stew meandered up my nostrils, bread in the hearth-oven wafted about the kitchen. I hadn't eaten since yesterday. Urgent calls for utensils, salt, water buckets, and every conceivable kitchen gadget imaginable was shouted for. The doctor took my arm. "This way."

I followed alongside, ever thankful for work, if any should come. An inside bed would be quite a find.

Right off from the hustle and bustle of the kitchen, the doctor tapped on a door. "Come."

The door swung open and there sat Mr Buffle, the very Buffle from London, from Lord Allenton's townhouse. I could never forget such a fat, ballooned red face, never. I swallowed, and then gulped for more air. Would he recognise me?

He stood. "Good afternoon, Dr Moore." He glanced at his mantle clock. "And right on time, I see, as usual." He sniffed the air.

"Mr Buffle, I wish to introduce Miss Wilson, she is looking for work. Might I add, she is excellent with animals. I can attest to that myself."

Good with animals? My heart almost stopped. I know nothing of animals other than to love them and kiss them and pet them and ..."

"That troublesome mare of Lady Sheffield's? Well, I believe Miss Wilson could have her settled within the week," said the doctor with an air of authority.

I gulped more air. *Me? Settle a troublesome mare? Oh, dear me. ...*

"Well, well, then," said Buffle eyeing my small frame as if I could not even lift a milk bucket. "We'll see, we'll see."

"Miss Wilson has a temperament to quell even the nastiest sort of cur, as well. She even hugged Hawkeye moments ago."

Mr Buffle's head jerked back. "Hawkeye? Impossible. Why you must be mistaken, doctor. That mongrel would bite his own leg if it weren't attached."

"She has a way Mr Buffle." The mantle-clock struck two gongs. "Oh, dear me, I must be going. Where is her ladyship?"

"In the study, sir."

The doctor turned to me. "Good luck, Miss Wilson."

"Good luck, Dr Moore." I frowned. "Excuse me, sir, I meant *best wishes.*"

He laughed. "It is of little matter." With that, he picked up his bag and left the room.

Mr Buffle resettled his grim face upon mine. "So ... you do well with animals, do you? Hmm, we'll see about that. Mrs Miles, the housekeeper, will settle you in a room. You'll start immediately—in the stables."

My room was beautiful and clean. One little bed, a cupboard and wash-basin sat along one wall. A roll was at the foot of my mattress, and neatly folded lay a great thick wool blanket. Oh, how fortunate I was at such a find, but what was I supposed to do now? Mrs Miles said I was to report to the stables within minutes.

I found my way into the yard and passed servants as they were setting up tents and tables. White netting was strung along from the rose trellis to the elm. The gardeners were shaving the thick, moist grass levelling the lawn into a great mass of well-shorn carpet. Chairs were stacked high, white tablecloths were folded and stacked neatly, the hum-drum of busybodies abounded in the afternoon air.

It was to be a spectacular wedding, I supposed. I walked along the stone path pausing to ask where the mews were located.

"Straight along the yew path, past the raspberries, follow the cobblestones and across from the carriage-house," pointed one of the maids.

As I meandered along following the direction, I was met by the same dog that greeted me earlier. This time he was growling, baring my path. The bristles on his neck were up, the thick collar snug around his neck was way too small, and I fancied uncomfortable for the raggedy old fellow.

"Hush now, ol' boy and come to me." I squatted meeting him eye to eye. "Come now, and let me loosen that collar." Still he growled as he cautiously approached, cocky and showing me his great, long teeth. "So, you're not old at all, by the looks of those white teeth. Come now, stop your bluster and let me make you feel better." I closed my eyes and reached out to him. His growl grew more intense. "Hush, now. Come and sniff my hand. I shan't hurt you. Come, sit."

He stopped growling. I kept my eyes closed and exposed the tender spot of my neck for his taking. With my hand still extended, I felt his wet nose touch the tip of my finger. "That's right, I'll not hurt you. Come along, we'll be great friends. I promise not to hurt you."

I opened my eyes, and his nose was inches from my face, his greyish-white eyes glaring into mine. He was sitting, and still came a low throated growl. "That's right, now you may lick my face." I smacked my lips, "Come now lick me."

His nose touched my cheek. I felt him sniffing my neck. When his nose came near my ear, his whiskers tickled, and I began to giggle. "Now laughing, I reached out and petted his head. "Good boy! We are friends now." Still giggling I ran my hand over his rough, mud-caked neck. "You are in need of a bath, my dear boy." Glancing around, I noticed the groom's wash-buckets stacked neatly along the stable's entrance. "Well, I do not know exactly what I am to do about this place, but I will start with bathing you."

The dog's tail wagged just a little. He wasn't quite sure if he wanted to really accept me. "Oh, in good time my friend, in good time." I petted his head. "May I remove that tight collar?" I leaned down to loosen it, but was met with a growl. "Oh, very well then, another day."

I had the dog all sudsy and dripping wet, when I was met by one of the grooms.

"Hawkeye, is it? No, I don't believe it. Ah, miss, don't know who ye are, but that dog ain't worth a bath—just a mean ol' scowl who thinks himself a bully. But, he's good around here at night. Nobody goes about him who don't know the stables. And who might you be?"

"Mr Buffle put me to work with the animals, sir."

"Doin' what?"

"Ah, I am not exactly sure. For one, I thought I'd settle her ladyship's horse. That is, after I bathe Hawkeye."

"Nobody settles *that* horse. That spirited misfit is to be sold, shot if ye ask my opinion. Never see'd such a disagreeable bit o' flesh."

"Oh, dear me. Well, perhaps she is just misunderstood."

He frowned. "Misunderstood? Well, now, that's a good one." He laughed as he shook his head. "Silly girl." His balding head was shiny in the sun's glare, his teeth spaced apart fit like a crooked old fence.

Hawkeye shook off, spotting my only frock. "Well, you might call me silly, but I'll show you. In which stall is this disagreeable mare?"

"Third one to the left. A black beauty, only beauty is to watch her flounce her self-importance. When you're not lookin' she'll kick ye brains out, twenty in the air. Beware missy, she'll show you something!"

"Well," I stroked the water from Hawkeye, and without

thinking, undid his collar. "I'll find for myself what you're saying." Now with the collar dangling from my hands, I noticed blood. Stooping down, I examined his neck. "Oh, dear me, that collar was troublesome to be sure." I let him sniff his collar, sniff the blood. "You see, you stubborn ol' boy that you have suffered for nought." He licked my hand. "Yes," I hugged his wet body, "you'll soon heal and feel all the better for it."

Hawkeye shook off again, and I dashed away laughing into the stables to find this misfit of a black beauty.

Glancing around, I found the stables cleaner and nicer than my room. The half-doors were burnished and shiny. The hard packed dirt floor had recently been swept—not a cobweb nor a bit of dust was leavened upon one thing. The windows were clear. The air, though musty with horse dung, was breathable and fit. Stable boys came and went, gardeners pushed their flower carts in and about the nickering of horses; the stomping and munching was a welcome noise filtered with the smell of fresh-shaved grass. *I love it here.*

Walking past each stall, I stopped. "So, there you are." Hawkeye nudged my leg. "No, not you, boy, but this black beauty is to whom I am speaking. "Hello, beautiful girl." The mare stood at the other side of her domain and eyed me with conquest, her rump shining in the warm sun, the shadow of her stall over her first half. Still chewing a mouthful of hay, she stopped. I noticed her nose sniffing my air.

"So, you are smarter than me, I can see that." I nodded. She nickered in agreement. "Will you allow me to enter your stall?" The mare backed up, uncertain of just who I was and what was I going to do to her. I unlatched her half-door and let myself in. Hawkeye eagerly pushed by me and hurried to the mare sniffing her muzzle. I could tell they were friends.

"Your name is a great one and matches you exactly." She sensed my sincerity and took a step closer, but just one step. "Raven, I find you more than beautiful. I surely do. Holly was black like you. Oh, how I loved her, but that was so long ago."

Hawkeye came to my side and sat. "Yes, Holly was a dog."

The mare backed up, now her entire body was in the sun. Her ears were perked, her large, well-set eyes sparkled blackish-brown, her lashes delicate and intricate. There was an activity in the stall next to her, Hawkeye and I joined by her side to find the matter. One of the stable boys led an old wagon horse into her stall. Her muzzle was white, grey whiskers sparse and prickly, her left eye white, her right eye black. Old welt marks lashed across her rump, similar to mine I mused. Her breathing was pained, I could see that. Raven nickered and tossed her head.

Watching the old mare, I sensed her bleak future. "Oh, dear ol' girl. I think you need a great rubdown, some oats, and fresh cold water." The old horse lifted her head and stared at me as if to question why I was in Raven's stall, and what was Hawkeye doing there with me.

I remembered seeing a bag of fresh oats hanging just outside Raven's stall. "Just a moment ol' girl." The black beauty followed close behind us. Curiosity always captivated the intelligent, and I noticed that about humans as well. "I'll be back, my black beauty, but first I must tend to that stable-mate of yours."

Hawkeye and I left Raven's stall, and I grabbed her bag of oats, and we let ourselves in the old horse's quarters. I noticed above her stall the name, "Sugar."

"Good afternoon, Sugar."

Hawkeye approached her with caution, sniffing. Raven held her head over the stable fence watching us intently, her ears pricked. Sugar swung her head to face us, her blind eye at our entrance. I had a curry-comb in one hand and the bag of oats in the other. "Hungry?" I scooped out a helping and held out my hand. The old horse sniffed the oats and eagerly began nibbling. I tied the loose fitting bag over her tired, droopy head. The fit was loose but functional.

Raven tossed her head. I offered her a handful. "Just this one time, your friend here needs them more."

Munching on her oats, the old mare stood straight with all four legs on the ground, perhaps remembering the day when she was brushed every morn.

It took a great while to untangle her mane, but once combed she looked rather proud. I then combed her tail and watched as she once more swished flies in grand fashion. Finding one of her hooves cracked, I searched the tack room and found an old rasp and file. On returning to her stall, she was standing next to Raven as if gloating at her new appearance. Raven's head was now hanging over the fence as she sniffed my hair. I felt her nibble at my bonnet as I held Sugar's hoof.

"Easy Raven, do not chew on my bonnet, it's the only one I have."

Just as I released Sugar's hind leg, Raven took a nip at my shoulder in a mean-spirited way. Jumping back I hollered. "No, Raven, bad girl!" She remained defiant, her ears pinned back, snorting. "Very well, then, *you'll get a taste of your own med-*

icine." [2] I climbed up next to her, firmly took hold of her bridle and pulled her head close to mine. Taking hold of her ear, I bit down on it, hard. She jerked back, her eyes flashing, her one ear flat against her head the other perked at me, she tried to free herself from my grip, but I wouldn't let her go so easily.

"There now, let that be a good lesson, rogue! Do not bite me again, Raven!" I scolded. I let go of her bridle and pushed her away in disgust. "You must learn your manners."

I finished filing Sugar's hoof and combed her down once more before leaving her stall. Raven was watching us all the while. I made sure Sugar's water was fresh and promised to return soon. "I will look after you Sugar girl." She trudged alongside me to the stall door.

Passing Raven's stall, she held her head over the half-door, but Hawkeye and I ignored the impudent great black beauty.

Now out into the sunshine, Hawkeye spotted something moving in the distant field and sprinted after it.

"So, I see you got a taste of her ladyship's horse?" said a stable boy.

"Oh, yes, she's a great beauty, but sorely needs to learn her manners."

"And you aim to teach her?"

I nodded. "It will take little time, I should think."

"That's it, little time. I've heard his lordship is to do away with the mare by week's end, after the wedding."

"Oh, I see. Well, maybe then I won't have enough time, but it is a shame, the mare is intelligent."

"Ay, she's that, I knowed for sure ... loves to bite, too."

I rubbed my shoulder. "I know."

"Ha! She's been at you, has she?"

"Yes, but I bit her back and she'll not repeat it on me again."

"Bit her back? Never heard of that one, never." He shook his head.

"She's a jealous creature, loves all the attention. Once she knows she's at the centre of it, she'll calm."

"Been around them all your life, have you?"

I thought for a while, *no but I've been kept in close quarters like a lot of animals for most of my life. I know how people cooped-up act, how they grieve, how they wish for freedom, to be loved and to love in return, yet scared to reach out, scared to*

---

2. Adapted from "The Cobbler Turned Doctor" in *Aesop's Fables* (Greece, 620 – 564 BC).

show their vulnerability, scared to show an inkling of trust lest they be mocked, beaten and discarded. I reasoned animals felt the very same way.

"No," I answered, "it is just that I treat all living things the very same way I wish to be treated. They understand far greater than we give them credit."

"Never heard of such thinking," he scoffed. "Talking to them creatures as if they be human. No, can't say I ever speak to 'em. Boss 'em about, but never ask them to do anything."

"Well, next time do ask them in a kind tone. They'll listen. It might take a while, but they'll grow accustomed."

"You some kinda animal doctor then, miss?"

"No. I just know the feeling of being unbridled, free to roam." I stopped talking; if I should by any means confess to being in prison, I'd not be trusted here.

"Might you be the new animal girl, Wilson?" said a servant all abreath rushing to my side.

"Well, I ..."

"Mr Buffle wants to see you this very minute."

What could he want? Had he recognised me after all? I walked back to the Great House with slow and deliberate steps. Hawkeye was nowhere to be found. I had not the time to dwell on Mr Buffle and what part he played by being at *this* Great House. How could I question why he was here, that would surely raise brows, for who was I to dare ask such impertinent questions?

Entering the servants' quarters, I went directly to his office. Knocking politely, I heard his voice.

"Come."

I entered. My head low, respectful, not sure at all what was to come.

"Lady Sheffield will ride this afternoon, Wilson. You will accompany her on Raven."

"Ride with her, sir?" I envisioned holding her waist as we straddled the horse. *Oh, dear me, I haven't the proper clothes.*

"Yes, that's right. You'll ride that old broken bag of bones stabled next to her horse."

I nodded. "Indeed, sir. I should be pleased to."

"It's not your position to be pleased or displeased, but to do as directed."

"Oh, indeed, Mr Buffle."

He eyed me for a second and then gestured for me to leave. "Two o'clock and I have no need to explain that you will be there promptly."

"No need, sir."

I left his office glancing down at my one simple frock, pinafore and day cap. *No, this would not do if I am to ride alongside her ladyship.* I asked one of the dairymaids where the housekeeper might be and was directed to the larder. There I found her counting jars of fruit.

"Madam, I have come in want of proper riding clothes. Mr Buffle informed me that I am to ride with Lady Sheffield this very afternoon."

"Ride with her?" Mrs Miles adjusted her spectacles and glared at me. "Why would you be chosen to ride with her? You're of little importance—I knew that from the very beginning."

"Indeed, Mrs Miles, but I suppose I was chosen because I am the new animal girl." I could feel my face burn. I found being a servant in such a great and grand house is work for people not fond of thinking, but of following orders explicitly and with an air of thankfulness and gratitude.

"Animal girl, indeed." She set down her paper and pencil. "Come along then."

I followed her upstairs into a part of the house I had no reason to have ever been sent. The floors were a bit dusty, though her hem skimmed most of it away as she hurried over the old oaken boards without care to the noise her clunky heels made.

At the very end of the long hallway, she stopped at the door. Taking up her dangle of keys, she inserted one into the lock and pushed open the door. It was musty and dark inside, save one large long window that shed a bright light across trunks, old blankets, hats, mannequins, and moulting furs that dangled around wire necks.

Mrs Miles rummaged through an open trunk and tossed me an old riding outfit, spiders scurried this way and that. With a shudder, I took the clothes, though they were those of a male servant, I understood exactly and promptly smiled at such a find. "Oh, these will do very nicely, ma'am."

"Put them on, let me see for myself."

I looked around for a bit of privacy."

"I haven't all day! Now put them on. I must see for myself if you look presentable."

I had to remove my clothes, what little I wore, and quickly Turning my back, I slipped on the trousers and quickly pulled the blouse over myself.

"What are those marks on your body?"

I froze. Those marks on my back were welt marks inflicted by the guards flailing a *pizzle* [3] when I'd struggle to be free of their grasp, but that was years ago. I hadn't any notion that marks were on my back.

"I ... I was whipped as a girl."

"Mouthy, eh?" She nodded. "I've noticed an impertinent air about you, what with your fancy words and way of speaking as if you were an educated lady." She sneered.

I faced her, trembling she might find me out. I must learn to speak ignorant. "Oh, ma'am, that be a year ago. I, I dunno remember." Standing upright I tried to fasten the trousers with a bit of old twine. "Will this do, Mrs Miles?"

She sniffed the air. "You stink. Wash and iron them, and while you're at it, clean yourself."

"Aye, ma'am." I quickly changed and grabbed the riding outfit and hurried from the room. I could sense the housekeeper, fat as a Sunday pig, envied my skinny frame and hated me all the more.

It was nearing two o'clock, and I had bathed and dressed. Not having a looking glass to see if I looked proper, I stopped the scullery maid. "Bessy is it?"

She looked up at me. "I be."

"My name is Wilson."

"I knowed, Grace."

"Well, I'm riding with her ladyship today and must look proper."

Her brows raised. Her ratty hair was tucked up under her white day cap, her teeth rimmed with black rot, her breath, foul. "Oh, now, ridin' with Lady Sheffield is it?" She cackled. "Well, you lookin' ever pretty than that ol' sow, Miz Miles."

I stepped back. "Oh, Bessy," I whispered, "you must not let anyone hear you speak so."

She shook her head and stood straight. "I knowed." She looked around with a sneer. "I be here since I were ... well, I be borned here. Look at me now, old. I knowed lots o' secrets, they ain't never leavin' *me* go."

I hugged her. "Well, Bessy, I don't know any secrets and must soon go before Mr Buffle or Mrs Miles shakes a broom at me."

She wiped the drool from her mouth and pulled me close. "No worries, pretty Gracie, later I'll tell ye a few secrets, so you's

---

3. Bull's pizzle; old English word for an animal part, used as flogging instrument. Circa 1523.

a keepin' your work here too."

"Oh, indeed, Bessy, indeed, but for now I must hurry, I cannot be late." I waved good-bye as I hurried out the door. *Secrets? I wondered just what secrets she had witnessed. Does she know Mr Buffle and his past? Would she know of Lord Allenton?*

Chapter 4 – The Animal Girl at Peabury

Hurrying out into the stable yard, my heart thundered in my chest. Oh, so much information in so little time. The word *secrets* kept my thoughts in a whirl. I was hurrying at such a great pace that I hadn't even stopped to wonder just where I was going. Hawkeye jumped to my side. "Well, hello ol' boy."

"I beg your pardon," came the voice of an elder gentleman sitting at the tea table in front of me. Looking me up and down, he adjusted his monocle. "Stableboy, is it?"

Looking up I didn't realise I had inadvertently entered the private garden of his lordship. Suddenly the old string around my waste broke, and my trousers slipped to my ankles.

"Ha ha ha!" came the old gentleman as he lifted his glass to salute me. "Ha ha ha!"

And for being addressed as a boy, I dropped my head and my voice, and pulled up my trousers. " 'Scuse me, sir." Turning quickly, I ran from the garden, Hawkeye at my side. *Oh, dear me, I must soon find a proper belt. So, I look like a boy?*

"Wilson," shouted the head-groom, Mr Snivel. He stood holding the reins to Raven. "Where the dickens have you been?"

Retying the string about my waist, I stammered, "My trousers, sir ..."

"Stop your gibberish and take Raven. The nasty animal tried to kick me again." He jerked hard on the reins. Snorting, the horse charged him. Her ears pinned back in defiance.

"Whoa, girl." I hurried over to Raven and took the reins from Mr Snivel, still clutching my trousers. "I'll take her, sir." Gently stroking her neck, I whispered, "Easy Raven girl, easy." The mare studied my face and sniffed my hair. "You remember, don't you?" She took a few steps back to give me another look. "Yes, you do," I whispered. "You must behave, or you'll be shot, quartered into horsemeat." I glanced down at Hawkeye, his mouth watering. "You see, he even knows it."

The mare's eyes—well set and wide apart—knew exactly my meaning. "Come along now. We'll have a word with Sugar before we take our ride."

Mr Snivel shook his head. "No time for that nonsense, Lady Sheffield is very impatient and has been waiting already by five minutes. Hurry along now, scrub."

I patted Raven's long silky black neck and whispered. "Some other time, my lady." I glanced at Mr Snivel. "Where's she waitin', sir?"

He shook his head as if I was an ignorant cast-off. "Carriage-porch, you ninny, where else?"

I nodded, mindful to keep my smart mouth to myself. "Aye, sir." I began walking straight on not at all sure where I was going. "Where is the carriage-porch, Raven?"

"Not that way," shouted Snivel. He pointed in the opposite direction, "past the garden, as you came in."

Hawkeye and I turned, and I followed alongside Raven as she led the way. "Thank you, black beauty. I'm really at a loss here. Do forgive me."

Raven and Hawkeye suddenly stopped. Looking around I spotted a well-dressed lady standing on the portico waving at us. "This must be the place." Hawkeye sauntered up the walk, wagging his tail as if he was to be invited along.

"Shoo away, hound," said Mr Buffle kicking at him. "Shoo away."

Hawkeye was a smart dog—a welcome at this venue was not to be his on this day. I chuckled as he pretended to be an ignorant cur and scurried under the yew a few feet away.

"When no one is looking, Hawkeye, follow us."

The dog lay down under the tree panting in the noon heat, his pink and black spotted tongue hung slimy and drippy. He chose to ignore the butler entirely, confident his day would come.

Ignoring me, Mr Buffle exchanged words with her ladyship just as Hawkeye aptly chose to ignore him. I stood holding the reins as her ladyship was helped atop Raven. "Behave yourself, girl," I whispered, "Hawkeye has not eaten lunch."

"That will be all, Mr Buffle," said her ladyship.

She watched him walk into the house. Looking me up and down, she held a quizzical face. "Mr Buffle tells me you're a young woman, Miss Grace Wilson, but your attire baffles me exceedingly. Why, you look like a little boy."

I squinted up into her face. "I be a girl, ma'am." I glanced down at my clothes and the measly string holding up my riding trousers. "Iffen me to ride along or walk next to ye, matters little."

She nodded. "Oh, just walk ahead, slowly." Exhaling lightly, she gently tapped me on the head with her riding whip. "I love Raven, Grace. And I love the name, Grace. Therefore, I am going to call you Grace, rather than Wilson."

Oh, very good. For a moment I thought she would call me Raven.

She slid her gloved hand down the mare's silky neck. "She is so graceful and intelligent." With a smile, she added, "more intelligent than I am, I suppose. His lordship is determined to do away with her, and I am determined to keep her."

I handed one of the reins up to her. "Your ladyship, Oh, indeed ... I mean no lettin' 'em do such a thin' to this great beauty, either. And to prove me notion, I won't let her do you harm." We moved ahead, past the entry gate and out into the soft churned soil of the bridle path. "Raven knowed I won't let ne'vr a wee bit of foolishness fro' her."

"Really, you know her disposition, then?"

I nodded. "Yes, ma'am and she knowed I knowed, with Hawkeye and me near abouts, that for sure."

She laughed. "Indeed. I've been watching you from the window, Grace. You have a way with them. I saw you bathe the hound; saw how you brushed Sugar. You know how to talk to them, don't you?"

I nodded.

"Teach me, will you?"

Hmm, I thought about such a thing, but didn't know how I could teach her about sharing from the heart; letting go, not being the butler, not being the lady, just being an equal. "Ah, ma'am, I dunno about such a thin' and how about doin' it."

"I can learn. Now, help me down, Grace."

"Yes, ma'am."

"Please, share your secret with me." She glanced towards the Great House. Frowning, she turned to me. "He's watching us." She exhaled deeply. "Let us move on."

"His lordship, ma'am?"

"Mr Buffle."

"Oh, indeed, ma'am, he watches everyone."

"I aim to show them I can ride as well as all the rest."

I was astounded, for a well-bred refined lady such as herself surely learned from an early age to ride proper. "Are you just learning then, ma'am?"

"Well, just last year I was thrown. The physician, Dr Moore, has been helping me recover from *that* most unfortunate experience. However, his lordship continues to worry over me."

I nodded. "You are very brave, ma'am."

She smiled down at me. "Oh, not so very brave, I assure you. I tremble every time I come close to a horse, particularly Raven."

"She was the one that threw you?"

"Yes, and I am to overcome it. I have my own mind, Grace."

"As you should, ma'am."

She drew back, surprised at my words when suddenly a wee smile followed with a nod.

"Very well, ma'am, I will help you, but I do not know how to explain my workings with these creatures. I simply put myself in their view. I treat them as equals, I don't tell them anything, I ask them in a quiet tone, curtsey even."

She nodded looking surprised. "Indeed, Grace."

"If they misbehave I growl, if they listen I smile and coo at them. That is all." I handed her the reins. "We'll return to her paddock, ma'am. I want to show you something." Raven and Hawkeye followed.

Her ladyship's eyes widened. "You see, they mind where you're going."

Once inside the stables, her ladyship walked alongside us. I was all amazement that she did not seem to fuss that her hem was catching filth with dung, mud, and urine. She never flinched once. "So, ma'am, you really do want to learn their ways."

"Indeed, I do."

Time was gentle upon her face, for she must be double my age. I judged her to be a kind, gentle lady of great insight—for a wealthy lady. I wondered how such a thing could be. I also knew the animals mistook her kindness for naivety and were sure to take advantage. That's what I had to explain to her.

When we came into the mews, I stopped at Raven's stall. "I want you to see something, ma'am."

Looking serious and intent, she nodded. "Indeed, do go on."

I removed the bridle from Raven and handed it to her. "I do not know the ways of making bits, ma'am, but I think this one is way too harsh on her mouth. Could you imagine having that much metal pressing on your tongue?"

"What is going on here?" Mr Snivel slammed the stable door behind him with a nasty push. "See here, you can't just ... oh, I beg your pardon, Lady Sheffield, I had no idea you were here."

"Do leave us, Mr Snivel, I am perfectly all right."

He looked at us with suspicion. "Yes, ma'am, but you do know how his lordship feels about *that* horse."

Her ladyship's face sobered, her dark eyes flashed, her words frosty. "Mr Snivel, I know very well the opinion of his lordship, now leave us."

He half bowed. "Very well, your ladyship." He glared at me. "Wilson, you will report to me when you are finished here."

"Aye, sir."

As he left the stall, her ladyship shook her head and turned once more to me. "Let me see that bridle, Grace." She examined the bit with a deep sigh. "Indeed, now I do understand. I would not want something so grotesque in my mouth either." She stared out from the stall into the lush green meadow. "This may have been the very bridle she was wearing when I was thrown."

"Are you heavy handed, ma'am?"

She nodded. "I suppose I am."

Raven nudged her.

We both laughed. "You see, she understands," I said.

Her ladyship took a step back. "Why, Grace, you speak as one educated, and just moments ago used an ignorant tongue. What of it?"

"Oh, ma'am, yes, my mother educated me, but to find work I must not speak with authority, higher-ups distrust me so."

She nodded, but I knew she did not know what I meant.

"Oh, your mother was educated, perhaps a governess, then?"

"I'm not sure, your ladyship. I was ten when I last spoke with her."

"Ten? Oh, dear me, how dreadful, Grace. You were but a little girl."

"And your age now?"

"Twenty and two, ma'am."

I hung my head praying she wouldn't ask me more.

"Yes, well then, shall we be about Raven? Show me how you would give her 'her head' as you say."

Smiling, I nodded. "She will love you for it, you'll see, ma'am."

"Well, then, I shall be more than delighted if you are correct."

She spoke as if she were a little girl, excited and happy."

"Now, then, your ladyship, please remove your gloves."

"My gloves?"

"I sense animals love the human touch, they know the difference." I ran my hand down Raven's neck. "She's a magnificent animal, wise and intelligent. She won't hurt you. I will go in search of a proper bridle." Hurrying back, I smiled. "I think this will do nicely."

Lady Sheffield examined it with doubt. "Perhaps ... but, Grace, it has no bit." She gave me a worried look. "Am I supposed to ride her without one?"

"If you are worried, ma'am, I'll ride her first."

"No, I will."

I smiled. "You have your own head, ma'am, as does Raven."

She gave me a quick look thinking me to be impertinent, but just as quickly changed her mind with a laugh. "Very well, sprite, perhaps you are right." She turned heading for the door. "Oh, I shall see for myself."

I put the bridle on Raven, and we left the barn. Once out into the lovely summer air, her ladyship giggled. "Help me up, will you?" she said excitedly. "Oh, finally excitement and wonder."

"First remove your gloves and pet Raven, ma'am."

Her face lost it sudden flush. "Oh, yes, indeed, I nearly forgot." She removed her spotless kidskin leather gloves and stuffed them into her riding jacket. "I am to rub her then with my naked hands?"

"Yes, Lady Sheffield, rub her neck then stand directly in front of her and let her look you in the eye. Let her sniff your hair, being mindful not to let her nip you. And if she does, you must nip her back."

"Nip her back? Why, I ..."

"You'd gain her respect, ma'am."

"Oh, indeed."

"Now then, whisper to her. As you stroke the softness of her muzzle tell her she is beautiful. Then let her sniff your hands."

She obediently did as instructed. "Now, please pet Hawkeye and let Raven sniff your hands. They are great friends. If Hawkeye trusts you, then she will as well. And for good measure, next time you'll pet Sugar."

Helping her up into the saddle, she looked unsure. "I do hope you are correct, sprite."

"Gently tug in one direction, ma'am. Say: Raven, please, to the right, Raven to the left, Raven stop. Use the reins to guide her."

"Oh, yes," she giggled, "oh, yes, I understand perfectly." With great ease and kindness she spoke: "Great black beauty turn right." She gently tugged on the right rein and Raven beautifully arched her neck and smartly turned right. "To the left, Raven," directed her ladyship with a great smile. "Grace, dare I take her out into the meadow?"

"Do you trust her, ma'am?"

"Oh, yes, I do." Sitting straight, she lifted her chin and took in a great breath. "Indeed."

"Then I would, gently at first. In the beginning, I think it prudent to keep petting her neck, talk to her with kindness. Let Raven choose the path. Ease on the reins, feel comfortable in the seat, ma'am. The mare knows far more than we do. Let her amble along … let her see the sky, let her stop for a sip now and again. Be firm yet gentle. Whisper to her. When you return, rub her back with your bare hands, and she'll love you forever."

"How do you know these things, Grace?"

I shrugged. "It just comes from my heart somewhere inside, ma'am. You have it, too, ma'am. Raven knows it, too. We both noticed." Hawkeye licked my fingers. "Now even the hounds know."

Tears sprang from her eyes. "Oh, do I?"

"Indeed," I smiled, "if you set your mind to it."

Why I took such impertinent liberties in speech to this lady I had never met before, even puzzled me. She could have me arrested and thrown back into prison, could have me marched off the property, stripped and beaten. I had no say so, no money, nothing. I was at everyone's mercy, but if Raven trusted her, surely I could.

With a grand smile, her ladyship turned Raven, and they sauntered out along the bridle path, into the sunshine, the mare's tail swishing, relaxed and contented, no doubt thinking she was in control.

"Just what are you doing?" Mr Snivel came into the side-yard. "What have you been saying to her ladyship? Making me look bad, saying things to make me look bad, have you? Want my job do you?"

"I be sayin' only how to ride the black beauty, sir."

"Well, you were supposed to ride alongside. His lordship is all in a knot that she rides alone on that black devil. If anything happens to her, you'll be the blame. Now get out of those ridiculous clothes and report to Mrs Miles."

"Yes, sir." I hurried out of the mews thinking I must soon leave and resume my trek to London. These were not friendly people here, excepting her ladyship and Bessy. Just as I reached the door, I heard Mr Snivel cursing Hawkeye, turning back I saw him kick the poor fellow in the head.

Hawkeye yelped and ran toward me, his right eye dangling from its socket. "Oh, God, boy."

I must have screamed loud enough to wake the dearly departed because everyone came running. I chased after poor

Hawkeye and found him huddling under a bush in the private garden of his lordship's, and just where the grand party would begin later this evening.

"Oh, dear God, Hawkeye, poor fellow, do come to me." Tears were running down my cheeks. "Let me help you, ol' boy." I cradled his poor head not knowing just what to do for him.

"Miss Wilson?"

Looking out from under the bush, I recognised the kind doctor who walked the path with me just a few week's past. "Oh, indeed sir, it is me. Please help this poor creature, sir," I sobbed.

He crouched down and squinted at us. "Dear me, indeed. Stay where you are, Miss Wilson. I will fetch my case."

Hawkeye and I remained under the bush until the kind doctor returned. By then guests had begun coming into the garden, and here I sat huddled under one of the hawthorns. *Well, I'll certainly be sent on my way for this.*

Just then the doctor reappeared. "Oh, sir, the poor fellow lost an eye," I said whimpering, "his eye!"

"Yes, I can see that."

Hawkeye growled. "Oh, dear boy, do not growl so, the doctor is good, and he will tend your wound." I stroked his head. "Easy boy."

"That's right, ol' boy, let me take a look."

"Patty, what is going on here?" The gentleman now standing over us was the very one I stood in front of earlier that day when my trousers dropped to my ankles.

"Oh, your lordship, one of your hounds has met with a boot."

Lord Sheffield snorted. "Well, perhaps you could remove the bloody hound to another place. Our guests are soon to be arriving." He stooped to get a closer look. "And what a ghastly sight you are there under that bush with that silly stable boy."

The doctor looked at me and smiled. "Yes, sir, I'll be one minute more."

"Yes, there's the little thief now." Mrs Miles pointed to me as she stood alongside his lordship.

Everyone in the garden stopped and stared.

His lordship straightened. "What? Mrs Miles lower your voice this instant, we have guests. Whatever you have to say, say it somewhere else. I'll not have a scandal ruin my son's wedding. Be off."

Mrs Miles took hold of my hair and dragged me from under the bush. "Indeed, we'll be off, sir."

"Mrs Miles," said the doctor, "what do you think you are doing?"

"Dr Moore, sir, she is a thief, and I have questions she alone must answer."

Lord Sheffield snorted. "She? Why, that young man is a stable boy. I saw him earlier with his trousers down."

"Trousers down?" She looked as if she would faint. "Oh, indeed, my lord, she is capable of all sorts of deceits, debauchery, and scandals. Imitations of all sorts is her card."

"Well, then, take her away this very instant." His lordship glanced around as the garden was fast filling with guests. "Hurry away."

Mrs Miles still had hold of my hair as she pulled me into the servants' quarters shoving me rudely into a chair. Bessy eyed me as she passed the open door.

"You'll tell me what you did with her ladyship's ring, Grace, Miss Wilson, or whatever your *real* name is."

I was stunned that Mrs Miles knew of my history, Mr Cooke's ring. How was that possible?

Just then the doctor entered.

"Oh, sir, how is Hawkeye?" I dropped my head into my hands and cried for the sadness of the poor beast.

"He's lost his eye, I'm afraid, but he'll live." He looked at Mrs Miles who stood with her hands on her hips, lips pursed; her face red and scornful. "What is the meaning of all this, madam?" His shirt, waistcoat, and trousers muddy and bloodstained from the dog.

"She's a thief, doctor. Stole a valuable ring, and I aim to prove it. Just look at the welt marks on her back. A *Wormwood Scrubs* [4] if there ever be."

I backed up against the wall. Everyone in the kitchen had stopped their clatter, all eyes were on me. The doctor looked puzzled. "A thief?" He looked at me. "Miss Wilson, what is the meaning of all this?"

"Sir, the marks on my back were inflicted years ago, ten and two, so I was. We were all beaten for doing nothing more than hiding from the guards."

Looking aghast, he eyed me with surprise. "Hiding from *prison* guards? Good God, what did you do?"

"Sir, I was accused of stealing Lady Allenton's ring."

Mrs Miles shouted, "Aha, you see, the little thief has repeated her deed! For now she has stolen our very own Lady Shef-

---

4. Old English slang for a prisoner. Circa 1850's.

field's ring, and just this afternoon."

My face drained pale. "Oh, yes, I was with Lady Sheffield today, but ... but. Oh, sir, you must believe me, I did not take her ring." I patted my pockets, searched the room, I wanted to run, but the door was blocked. I could not be put away for another ten years. Tears sprung from my eyes. I dropped to my knees pleading, "Oh, good sir, please believe me."

Just then Lady Sheffield entered the kitchen, Bessy at her side. "Mrs Miles, who gave you permission to question Grace?" Her face was red, her eyes teary. "She has done nothing wrong!"

"Why, your ladyship, you yourself said your ring went missing while out riding this very afternoon. I simply concluded that this little prisoner was the thief. She just admitted to a prior arrest for stealing a ring." She grabbed me by the shoulders, spun me around and ripped off my blouse. "See for yourself her prison welts."

In horror, I turned to hide my nakedness.

"You see?" Mrs Miles lifted her chin mightily. "See for yourself the marks on the wretched thief's back?"

Lady Sheffield hurried to my side and covered me with her shawl. "Oh, poor girl, I am so sorry." She turned to her personal maid. "Miss Mercy take Grace to my room and have her bathed and clothed. Use my things as necessary."

The doctor stood in the corner, stunned at such happenings. I dared not look him in the eye. Keeping my head down, I wept, ashamed of what I had done—but I had done nothing wrong.

Lady Sheffield put her arms around me and faced everyone. "While Grace so kindly instructed me to ride 'the wild beast' she instructed me to remove my gloves, 'to better feel the animal,' she said. I did, and in doing so pulled my ring off. I later found it in my glove."

I exhaled deeply. By now my eyes were puffy and red. I heaved a huge sigh of relief. "Oh, ma'am, thank you. I am so sorry."

"You have nothing to be sorry about, Grace." She turned to the housekeeper. "You are dismissed, Mrs Miles. You will leave these premises immediately."

I was escorted out of the room by Miss Mercy, just then Mr Buffle met us in the doorway, his face puffed, his brows high, so self-assured, indeed. "Well, well, the animal girl has found trouble again, so you did. I might have ..."

"Enough of your misguided opinions, Mr Buffle," said Lady Sheffield. "I have let go Mrs Miles; another word from you and you'll be next." She fumed. "And I want to see Mr Snivel this very instant."

Mr Buffle's face turned crimson. "Yes, ma'am, I'll bring him immediately. May I inquire as to the interrogation, ma'am?"

"No, you may not."

He left the room, and everyone turned back to their duties. Bessy found me in the hall and hugged me. "I be sorry, Miss Gracie girl, 'bout ol' Hawkeye and yeself."

I kissed her cheek. "No worries, Bessy, I'll be all right. Hawkeye will survive."

"Come, Miss Wilson," said Miss Mercy, "I'll have a nice bath readied for you."

"Miss Wilson," said the doctor, "forgive me for interrupting your retreat, but I would like to speak with you this evening, if it is possible? You mentioned a Lady Allenton and ..."

"Oh, yes, sir." I prayed he might know of the same family and would have questions that could be answered. "Sir, as soon as I am dressed proper, I'll find you, sir."

A kind smiled enveloped his face. "But of course, so sorry for the nasty accusation, Miss Wilson, so very sorry."

"Oh, sir, it is no fault of yours. You've been all kindness. I just hope I haven't embarrassed you in front of so many."

He took my hand. "No, Miss Wilson, you did not. Go now, rest."

Chapter 5 – Poppy and Lady Sheffield

Now bathed and dressed in the finest silks, with my hair washed and done up, with purple velvet ribbons entwined in my braids I felt as if I were in heaven. Even my hands looked pretty. Well, I wasn't exactly sure just how pretty ... perhaps nice and clean with my nails now filed properly.

I found a long looking-glass and was stunned to see myself for the very first time in such detail. Walking up close, I examined my face. "Well, it is freshly washed, shiny and well proportioned—my eyes set large and dark-brown. Yes, I have grown. I must look like my father, for I do not resemble Mama at all. My hair was bright red and very curly, Mama's was black and straight.

"Yes, indeed," said someone from behind me, "you look quite lovely in lavender. It is my favourite as well."

Turning, I found Lady Sheffield. "Oh, ma'am, how can I thank you for all of this?"

She took my hand. "I thank *you*, Grace." She glanced at the mantle clock. "I must rejoin the wedding ball for my son Andrew and his wife, Elizabeth. You must come with me."

I was stunned. I was to mingle with her company? "Oh, Lady Sheffield, I will embarrass you, I am sure of it."

She laughed. "Oh, I hardly think so. Anyone with such a loving heart cannot possibly embarrass anyone. You must tell me all about your *past* life, Grace. Tomorrow morning we shall have tea." She glanced at the mantle clock. "Come along now, I have been absent far too long." She took my hand. "Come, come."

We entered the ballroom. I hesitated, thinking the music would fade ... fearful and expectant that everyone would turn and gape, that they would stare at me, point and whisper, and in disgust, turn away, surely. However, to my amazement, I was ignored. Her ladyship garnered all the smiles and nods. I melded into the crowded room looking no more or no less grand than any of the other ladies. *So, they do not recognise the animal girl.*

Her ladyship whisked me along, her giggle now a familiar

note to her natural ways. Shortly, I was introduced to her husband, a tallish, portly sort of gentleman, sandy-grey hair, monocle in his right eye, a quick smile. Lord Sheffield, indeed. I had met him earlier that morning—in the garden. I prayed he wouldn't recognise me as the stable boy with loose trousers.

Glancing at me, up and down, his lordship shook his head with a smile. He removed his monocle. "Well, well, yes, how very nice to meet you, *Miss* Wilson. Indeed, her ladyship said she had worked a miracle."

"A miracle, sir?"

"That she turned a young trouser-less stable boy into a beautiful young woman."

I could feel my face burn crimson. His lordship laughed.

"No worries, Miss Wilson, you're a better sight now than earlier this morning. Ha ha ha."

"Thank you, sir." I curtsied.

I was offered a glass of champagne and took it—not wanting to look ignorant. Dear me, I had never drunk anything before in my life. Sipping it, I was disappointed at its bitter, sparkling taste. The quaint little bubbles spiralling to the top, though, were quite amusing, tickling the insides of my mouth.

"And what has become of your hound?"

"Hawkeye, sir?"

"He will live, your lordship," said a man's voice behind me. "I just left him growling moments ago. His head wrapped like a kettle of fish."

A kettle of fish? Turning I found the kind doctor, Dr Moore. His unassuming smile caught my breath. I frowned and then suddenly unfrowned and took another sip. "Oh, yes, Hawkeye." Feeling ashamed at abandoning the dear boy, I apologised to the good doctor. "Oh, thank you sir, I haven't had a moment to myself, else I would have his head cradled on my lap this very moment."

He glanced into my face with a warm smile. "Wearing that beautiful gown?"

I glanced down at my fine silk lace handkerchief, nervously twisting it. I felt the soft, warm curl of braids resting upon my bare shoulders. "Well, sir, I suppose not in this ..." I felt a warm sensation move through my body. It must be the champagne. *I am the animal girl, how silly I must appear in her ladyship's clothes.* I glanced over at his lordship. "Sir, I am more than honoured to have been invited to this lavish ball." I sighed deeply. "I am the animal girl and cannot for a moment imagine why I have been invited here."

"Animal girl, indeed." They both smiled.

His lordship looked down at me squinting from his eyeglass. "Miss Wilson, you really should learn to smile more, it would become you."

"Your lordship, I fear Miss Wilson does not smile for being worried about the hound." The doctor turned to me. "Miss Wilson, Hawkeye is quite comfortable at the moment. He is situated in a warm bed of straw. I've personally seen to it."

"Oh, sir, your kindness to such a lowly creature is to be commended. Thank you, sir."

His chest swelled, his face glowed even through his tanned, freshly shaven face.

"That's why he attends her ladyship, Miss Wilson," said his lordship. "If such a man considers a lowly hound, he must think my wife a goddess."

They both laughed.

"Yes, and besides all that, our kind and well-mannered doctor is my nephew. What say you, Patrick?"

Nodding, he smiled. "That I am, sir, and very fortunate at that. "And I wonder just where Cousin Andrew and his bride have wandered off to?"

His lordship's face crinkled as he glanced around the room. "Well, you know, Andrew doesn't mingle well."

"So he does not." Dropping his voice, Dr Moore smiled at me while nudging his lordship. "Sir, on a serious note, I have much to discuss with Miss Wilson and beg your leave."

Lord Sheffield removed his monocle with a nod. "Very well, Patty, very well, but mind your Aunt Catherine is anxious to speak to you regarding something or the other."

"Oh, sir, I won't be the evening, I promise. I also want to find Andrew and Elizabeth and extend my blessings."

"Oh, indeed, my boy. We shall see you then very shortly." He nodded to me. "Good evening, Miss Wilson."

I curtsied (not at all certain I was to do such a thing.) "Good evening your lordship."

As Dr Moore escorted me out onto the balcony, I felt the cool air float about my neck. The night sky was purple velvet; a swirl of pinkish, orange clouds surrounded the setting sun. The clink and clatter of glasses, the silvery tones of female voices muted as the doors closed. "It is lovely here, sir."

Dr Moore took in a great breath. "Ah, indeed, Miss Wilson it is. I am glad we are alone." He turned and stared up at the full moon. "I am the second son to Lord Allenton, miss."

His son? I was astounded. How could I have wandered along an unknown path to Peabury and be joined by the very family I was in search of. Impossible. I remained silent and very confused.

"I was *'a late birth'*, as they say. There were ten years between my brother, George and myself. We were never really close. I have no idea where he or my mother are at the moment, neither have written in a very long time."

"Oh, sir, I am sorry to hear of it."

He smiled down into my face. "I know." He paused. "Lady Sheffield is my Aunt, she took me in, so to speak, Miss Wilson. She is my mother's sister—Mother has not written to her either." He lamented. "Estranged, one would suppose."

I nodded not knowing exactly what to say. I knew the word estranged meant they were separate. How well I knew the word separate.

"Without her, I would have had no family at all. She is the dearest angel on this earth."

"Oh, her ladyship, Lady Sheffield, then? Here at Peabury?"

"The very one. She's more a mother to me as Lord Sheffield is a father." He turned to me. "Now, please explain about this ring you supposedly *stole* that landed you in prison."

I knew I could not say a word regarding what really happened until I was very sure of myself. "Well, sir, I shall go back to the very beginning. I faintly remember a young gentleman accompanying Lord Allenton in the garden in London ..."

"The London house, yes ... near ten years ago, it would have been me. I would have been twenty at the time. Father loved his flowers. We spent many happy hours there."

"Do you remember a little flower girl named Poppy?"

He glanced back up at the moon. "Hmm, Poppy?" He frowned in concentration. "I remember a little red-headed waif at the gate with a fistful of ..."

"Daisies, white daisies, sir," I smiled. "I am Poppy. At least that is what everyone called me, then."

"You don't say?" Turning to face me he smiled. "I would have never imagined such a coincidence, Miss Wilson. So, you knew us then?"

"I remember his lordship. He would always buy my flowers. Mama cleaned your mother's shoes."

"You lived close by, then?"

"In an alleyway, sir, a very long distance—for a little girl and my dog, Holly."

He nodded. "Well, yes, that was long ago. Father was much older than Mama. He began to forget things, became more and more confused. My brother George would become frustrated with him. George was always short-tempered. Someone found Father wandering about one night and rescued him. He was nearly run-on by a wagon.

"Then while away at Cambridge, I was notified that he had apparently wandered off again in the fog. This time the constable said he no doubt fell into the Thames. I rushed home, but found nothing more regarding his disappearance. Years later, he was declared dead in absentia. George, of course, inherited the title, the estates, all the wealth. George and Mother sailed to America the following year, leaving nothing behind but me. "I finished Cambridge and became a physician."

Though I had a very strong feeling about the kind doctor's brother and mother, I knew my suspicions would only lead me into further trouble. Who would ever believe my story of his lordship being tied up, taken to jail, the poor soul probably died there or in some foreign country. I envisioned the silver glitter of the beautiful diamond ring of Mr Cooke's. I remember the name O'Malacy as the policeman who arrested his lordship and me ... he took Mr Cooke's ring. Was he the one who had pronounced his lordship drowned in the Thames?

"Then one day I received a letter ..."

"A letter, sir?"

"From my mother, if you can imagine such a thing after such a long absence."

"Oh, dear me, no, I could not imagine such a thing."

"Well, she was broke. My brother gambled his fortune, sold his title and ..."

"Sold his title, sir? How can that be?"

"It can't. He must have been desperate and the fellow he sold it to a simpleton. I cannot wait to meet this American when he comes to England to claim his castle."

"Oh, indeed, sir. How unfortunate for the American, I must say."

"Serves him right."

"Oh, indeed, sir."

"Well, I sent my mother all my savings. The money I was going to use to set up my practice."

I nodded feeling sympathy for the very kind doctor. "I know very well how it must feel to be handled in such a rough fashion and to lose contact with your mother ..."

"Oh, Miss Wilson, forgive me. I've been prattling on so when I can only imagine what you've been through. Why, I have no right to go on so."

"Oh, sir, you have every right. My life is my own." I took in a great breath. "And I must soon be on my way to London, to reclaim my reputation, for I've done nothing wrong."

"No, you have not, Miss Wilson, but you were explaining about the ring. Please go on."

"Well, the ring was a beautiful thing to behold, silver with a very large diamond in its centre. Oh, I remember it quite well. It was almost blue." I explained about taking her ladyship's shoes to Lord Allenton's great house, meeting Mr Cooke, leaving and getting lost in the fog. I explained how I encountered Mr Cooke again that day and how Mama came searching for me and found me having tea with him. He walked us home that night. While putting his coat over my shoulders, the ring must have slipped into my apron pocket.

Dr Moore nodded. "Mr Cooke was father's butler. And, if I remember correctly, his mother was my mother's nanny."

"Indeed, Dr Moore. Well, I was in search of him with his ring in my apron pocket when a policeman came up behind me in the alley, very near your great house. Questioning me at length, I handed up the ring as proof of my endeavours, but he immediately accused me of stealing such a gem, and I was marched off to jail. "That is all I recall, sir." *I knew I could not let on about the skulduggery that really took place, what good would it do? I was determined to find the answer and explain it all to the kind doctor in good time.*

"I see," said Dr Moore, shaking his head. "I know London is rife with little beggars, pickpockets, and thieves of every age, but … you, of all people. Why they put you in prison for over ten years? You were much too young."

"Ah, that is the very question, sir."

"Well, Poppy, as I see it, if it weren't for my family, you'd probably be a happy little flower girl somewhere in London with lots of smiling babies of your own." He turned to me. "Please, you must allow me to help you."

Just then a couple approached from behind, it was the newly married couple. "Patty," his cousin whispered with a nervous laugh, "do find a way for Elizabeth and me to escape—it's Mother, you know."

Dr Moore chuckled. "Indeed. Well, I suppose I could say I have diagnosed a severe case of *Romeo-Julietism* and had to confine you both to your room. But before I do such a thing, you must first meet Miss Wilson." He turned to me. "Miss Wilson, allow me to introduce you to my cousins, Mr and Mrs Andrew Mason, recently married by two hours."

I curtsied. "Oh, indeed. Very pleased, I am sure." My tongue felt as if it were tied in knots. I could feel my face begin to burn. I dropped my glance, feeling so very privileged to meet this most elegant couple. I dared not be so bold as to look directly into their eyes.

Taking my hand, the newly married Mr Mason smiled. "Oh, indeed, the animal girl—Miss Wilson. You have impressed Mother entirely. So very pleased to meet you, I am sure." His grasp was warm and sincere.

His bride nodded. "Oh, yes, Miss Wilson, animal girl, indeed." She gushed. "I so love all God's creatures. You must teach me how to speak to them." She took my hand. "Promise?"

I drew back. *How quickly word has spread about me. What if they find out I am a sham and know very little regarding animal behaviour. Would they label me a fraud along with the other charges lodged against me already?* "Well, ma'am, I, I ..."

"Very well, then," said Dr Moore, "I will quarantine the two of you this instant. Now then, be off with you. I'll tell Aunt Catherine of your affliction."

Andrew laughed. "Mother will be disappointed with you Dr Flimflam, I am sure of it," he laughed taking his bride's hand. "Thank you, Patty."

"Goodnight, Patrick," said the new bride as she kissed his cheek.

"Goodnight Mr and Mrs Mason."

We watched them hurry away into the dark night, holding hands, laughing.

Just then Mr Buffle came out onto the balcony and passed me by without notice. *He doesn't recognise me either. As a matter of note, none of the household servants recognised me.*

"Dr Moore, I am puzzled. Mr Buffle, just moments ago, walked past me without notice."

"Butlers are *trained*, my dear."

"Trained? Oh, you mean to be discreet?"

He nodded. "This afternoon he was nearly let go. I wager he will treat you with the utmost respect henceforth, Miss Wilson."

"Dr Moore, I have no idea why her ladyship has dressed me so, or why she has taken me under her wing. I feel ... undeserving."

"She has taken a great liking to you, Miss Wilson. You know you are a kind and sincere young lady. And," he chuckled, "you have the same bright red hair that matches my mother's, to a tee, I must say."

"Oh, indeed, sir." I fondled one of my curls. "Your mother is her ladyship's sister, Lady Sheffield? Well, perhaps because of my red hair she has taken such a fancy to me." Looking down at my elegant attire, I clasped my hands. "I have most recently, by a month, been set free from prison. The clothes I wore just this very afternoon were given to me by them to start my new life. It's hard to imagine such kindness."

"Indeed, Miss Wilson. And now you are starting a new life for yourself."

"No, sir, I cannot start a *new* life as simple as that. I must first earn my way."

"Earn your way, pray tell? You said you were innocent of the charges, served your time, and now you are free. What more is there to make of it?"

"My reputation, sir. I must return to London and find my mother." I glanced around. "And, I must find Cooke."

He took a step back. "Cook? Dear me, Miss Wilson, allow me to bring you a plate. You must be famished."

"Oh, no sir, not the cook, but Mr Cooke, sir, but I thank you." Just then Mr Buffle came back out instructing one of the servants to attend us. I turned away, not wanting to tempt fate, if such a thing could be.

"Here you are, Miss Wilson." The kind doctor handed me a glass and took one for himself.

Buffle moved on, either pretending not to notice me, or as the doctor said, 'trained.'

"Sir, I ..."

He put his fingers to his lips, whispering, "Wait until he is out of sight." We watched Buffle disappear into the ballroom.

"That look on your face, Miss Wilson, do you suspect Mr Buffle of something? Was he associated with Mr Cooke?"

I swallowed hard, thankful we were not in the direct glow of lights, for my face would have given me away. It was useless to involve Dr Moore further in this sordid affair. Sadly, his father was no doubt dead by now, but I would find that out for myself, and if I should find my mother or Mr Cooke, perhaps then I could sort everything out and have something of real value to present to the good doctor.

Looking up at him, I shook my head. "I do not know if Mr

Buffle remembers me, sir, but perhaps someday I will find out."

He sipped the last of his champagne and set down the empty glass on the balustrade. "Well, yes, it was long ago, and I would just as soon forget the entire episode regarding my mother and brother, that is. My dear father, however, is another story."

"Oh, there you are, Grace," said her ladyship fluttering to my side. She nodded to Dr Moore. "Well, better company could not be found. You are safe with my dearest physician, but do come in and talk to me about animals. I am bored, my dear, terribly bored."

"Oh, indeed, your ladyship." I smiled and nodded adieu to Dr Moore. "Good evening, sir."

"Good evening, Miss Wilson. Perhaps we'll meet over breakfast."

I smiled and followed her ladyship into the ballroom. I had made up my mind that I would set off for London earlier rather than later. It was a full moon. I shall leave at 3 o'clock in the morning. I should do very well in the quiet of the night and sleep during the day. I had made many friends here, but worried more so for Hawkeye. However, I knew the doctor would take very good care of him. Perhaps someday I would return. I felt a deep fondness for Raven and Sugar, and Lady Sheffield.

That night her ladyship and I talked on and on about many things. I confided in her about all that had transpired in my life thus far (except about Lord Allenton) and that I would be leaving in the early morning hours—I needed to clear my name—needed to find my mother. She offered her carriage, offered to accompany me, offered me very much money, but I refused.

"Ma'am, please, if you would, explain to Dr Moore that I had to go. It is a sad thing to say good-bye."

"Indeed it is, Grace. You know Patrick will fuss, he's grown quite fond of you."

"Indeed, ma'am. He's a fine doctor."

"Well, I too shall miss you. Once in London, you must write to me."

"I will, and someday I shall return to Peabury, I promise."

Chapter 6 – Poppy Leaves for London

My first night alone after leaving Peabury was on the London Road, and it turned out to be startling. I had walked until dawn had just begun to break, and when I stopped to prepare a fire for my breakfast, I heard a noise in the bushes. Being alone, I was always concerned about highwaymen. With my heart in my throat, I cried, "Who goes there?"

Scooting back from the fire, I grabbed my purse and sat on it. "Who goes there?"

Pushing through the bushes, to my amazement grunted Hawkeye, his head still well-wrapped. He wiggled in delight at finding me. "Well, well, my boy," I hugged him laughing and crying all at once, "how did you find me, dear boy?"

He licked my face and whined as if he hadn't seen me in months. "Now, now my silly boy you must have a sip of water. I tried to examine his bandages to make sure they were still in place, but there wasn't enough light. "The sun is soon in coming, dear boy. I shall then examine your head." I poured him a dish of water and gave him what few bites of what food I had. "Go on now, ol' boy, you must eat."

He looked at the food and then back at me. "Go on, I've had my breakfast."

As if shrugging, he lapped up his dish of water and consumed his few morsels and then turned in a circle and lay down. I examined his paws for thorns, but they were tough as new leather. "You've got thick paws, my boy. You'll do well by my side, for we have many rough miles ahead to travel. I can't go back to Peabury to return you ... not just yet, anyway."

I lay my head on his body and slept. When I awoke, the sun was atop my head. There was a lovely stream nearby in which to bathe. I found my purse, and as I always do, counted my money. To my surprise, when I opened it I found a wad of money tied with string. Rummaging a little further I found a note and a card.

My dear Grace, if at any time you need my assistance, financial or otherwise, you must only mention my name and present my card. When you return to Peabury, we shall sort it all out. God's speed. I look forward to your return. Lady Sheffield.

Dumbfounded, I counted the money. It was a fortune to be sure. I had a mind to send it back, but realised she wanted me to have it. Under my present circumstances, being overly proud was not at all appealing. Besides, I rather think she was sincere in wanting to come along with me to find my mother. There must be some women in the world who are mothers ... mothers to children everywhere, no matter who birthed them. Lady Sheffield was such a woman. I would learn to love her as my own. I felt that in my heart. Kissing Hawkeye, I patted his head gingerly. "Ol' boy, you've stumbled into the lap of luxury."

Standing, I stretched and took in a great breath. "Indeed, we'll walk to the next town and find a coach to London, but you must behave, Hawkeye. No growling, stealing bones, or being ungentlemanly. You must promise." I glanced at his one eye as he peered up at me, his stubby little tail wiggled. "I'll even find the nearest apothecary and have him tend you." I petted him fondly. "You'll do, old boy, you'll do."

* * *

When we arrived in the small town of Croydon, but ten miles south of London, I right away inquired about an apothecary where I might have Hawkeye attended to properly.

We found an old gentleman who found Hawkeye to be healing nicely. I was taught how to clean and wrap his head. Not a pleasant sight, I assure you. I do not take well to sickness or injured creatures of any sort, but in this case, I had no choice.

The second thing I did was buy myself some very nice frocks, bonnets, and boots. I even bought a proper collar and a fine, braided leather leash for Hawkeye.

I found a very nice room at The George Inn and garnered food enough for a nice meal for us both. I tossed my old clothes into the corner and dressed myself proper. There was a small looking glass on the table, and I peered at myself with a smile. Hawkeye pawed my new frock.

"No, no, you must not spoil my good looks." Smiling down at my friend, I curtsied. "I say, my dear boy, you must agree that I do look quite respectable, all in all. But I am not sure exactly what to make of *you*. At any rate, the next stagecoach leaves for London in the morning, and we'll be on it, bandaged head and all."

The very next morning, with Hawkeye's head re-wrapped (not as nicely done as the apothecary's) we set off for a nice breakfast. I must have looked convincingly elegant, as the other ladies and gentlemen nodded, smiled and made way for me as we descended the stairs into the lobby. Once into the breakfast room, I was immediately situated at a lovely window table. No one remarked about Hawkeye as he obediently lay by my side, though wisely nearer the wall. While being served, I could watch out the window for our coach and sneak a tidbit for my grateful companion.

A hotel man entered the room and called out, "London coach. Passengers will board half-past ..."

Sitting up, I quickly finished my tea and sweet cakes. I would prepare myself to find a good position in which to board the coach. I had already given over my portmanteau and only had Hawkeye to tend. Taking in a great breath of fresh air, I stood waiting for the coachman's instructions. Presently I was handed up into the coach with Hawkeye close to my side. I was first in and took the forward seat, Hawkeye to my side, hidden by the fullness of my skirt. I was gazing out the window and did not notice the man who took the seat across, but Hawkeye did. He lunged at the man with such a ferocious growl and snapping of teeth as to even scare the toughest soul. By my word, who was the man sitting directly across but Mr Snivel himself. Oh, I thanked my lucky stars that the leash I had wrapped around my wrist held Hawkeye only inches from his face.

My scream must have startled the dog, for he backed down, but his teeth were still very visible, long and white, his spittle banged about my wrist. Mr Snivel was pasty white as his head was now flat against the coach wall, his hat tumbling onto the lap of the gentleman next to him.

"Ma ... madam," he shouted, "hold that beast this instant!"

Mr Snivel did not recognise me at that moment, but I saw the glimmer of recognition soon spread over his face as he looked at Hawkeye and then to me. "Madam, you will restrain that beast as I depart, if not I will have to take matters into my own hands."

"And, what sir, might that be, kick his other eye out?" I tried to soothe Hawkeye. I didn't want his eye to begin bleeding again. "There now, ol' boy, do calm yourself. He's not worth the effort."

The gentleman who sat next to Snivel inched his way from the coach as well and jumped out. Scowling his immense displeasure at the ruckus, he chided Snivel "Kicked his eye out, sir?

Why, what a cruelty, to be sure."

Snivel plopped his hat back atop his head. "If I had my way I'd have done him in on the spot, lost my job to that worthless cur."

By then, a crowd had gathered to witness the turmoil. I finally calmed Hawkeye and made him lie at my feet. I hid him best I could with my skirt, all the while, holding a most delicate and sophisticated look ... as if I were a lady in waiting to the Queen. I did manage to ask the coachman in a very haughty tone as to just when the coach would be leaving, saying I had many calls to make in London and I had not a moment to spare.

We left Mr Snivel standing on the boarding platform, his hat a bit dented; his pride more so. Loosening the leather leash around my wrist, I noticed it was now swollen red and no doubt bruised. *I must buy longer gloves.*

When we arrived in London, it was well into the eighth hour of that evening. I was not at all sure where we were, but knew well enough to take a room and sort out the next day's search well rested and well fed. Upon inquiries, I was escorted to the Mivart Hotel, Brook Street, Grosvenor Square. I found it quite proper for the likes of Hawkeye and myself, so listed in the Royal Blue Book, or Fashionable Directory left conspicuously in the lobby. "Indeed, this will do quite nicely."

I kept track of every penny spent thus far. I would repay Lady Sheffield, and in person. I thought of the good doctor, Dr Moore, and felt shame in not leaving him a note. He was so very kind to Hawkeye and me. Oh, if I could only find out about his father, perhaps find the policeman O'Malacy ... well, that would be tomorrow's fare.

Upon awakening, I found rain pattering on the window. Thunder rolled far off in the distance. Hawkeye had hopped atop my bed. "I know, I don't like it either, my friend." Glancing about the room, I had forgotten to buy an umbrella, but as luck would have it, someone left theirs hanging on the coat-rack. "Perhaps, I shall borrow it, then."

While I dressed, Hawkeye stared at the door, his ears perked; his nose sniffing what must be strange new smells. "You know, you're remarkably calm, my boy." I patted his head. "And remarkably well-mannered for such a brute, though your outward display of distaste for Mr Snivel is certainly understandable, I wish it of you to remain a little more refrained. Will you? It shall make my days so much more enjoyable."

He grunted.

"I will re-bandage your head, and then we'll soon be out-of-doors, and you can do your business. And then I will find my way ... I, at least, think I will find my way back to my home in the alley."

Chapter 7 – Inspector Peter Palgrave – Scotland Yard

As Hawkeye and I left the Mivart, the rain suddenly stopped, but I kept the umbrella open as we continued down Great Russell Street, past the Museum. The sky was still very grey with white patches coming and going. The walks were still shiny from the rain as I hip-hopped over the puddles.

My line of questioning was met with polite nods instead of disdain and rude rebuffs. Well, I really must look like a lady. In my thoughts, I had thanked her ladyship many times over for the money she gave me. I could now afford to conduct my investigations appearing to be a lady of means, one used to having her way. I think perhaps I could have been a very great actress.

Still pondering my thoughts as I found Parliament and the Thames, which gave me a sense of direction. I faintly recalled the bakery where Mr Cooke sheltered me the evening I got lost, but on what street and what was its name? Where was the alleyway?

My feet were beginning to blister from my new boots, and while situated in a small café, I slipped them off. Yes, I remember his lordship's home, two streets from the Thames. Closing my eyes, I remember running up an alley, finding a gate ... yes, the gate to his lordship's great townhouse. Oh, if I had only asked Dr Moore where his home was located exactly, how much easier the discovery.

I wondered if Mother would recognise me, now looking quite the lady. Perhaps she's one of the patrons sitting about this little café. I must have been staring at the lady sitting across from me, for she smiled with a nod, her daughter sat stiff and proper, dressed as a doll.

"I say, are you waiting for someone in particular?" she asked setting her teacup to its saucer.

Her daughter glanced down at Hawkeye and petted his head. "Good boy."

"Oh, yes, indeed I am searching for my mother. Might you

know of a certain Mrs Helen Wilson, very near Lord Allenton's great house?"

"Lord Allenton?" she looked at me in such a way. "Why, I have no idea where he lives, miss. And I have never heard of Mrs Wilson. Sorry to say." She shifted in her seat. "Are you travelling alone, miss?"

Knowing it improper to do such a thing, I shook my head. "Oh, my no, Mr Hawkeye lies in waiting this very moment."

"Oh, well then, but of course."

Her daughter smiled at me as she tugged at her gloves. "We must be going, Mama. Papa will be waiting for us at the museum entrance."

They stood, smiled at me, and bid me good day. The lady's daughter stooped and said goodbye to Hawkeye. Standing, she nodded at me with a sweet smile. "Good day, Mrs Hawkeye."

I watched them leave and felt very much alone. Even that little bit of conversation was a comfort. Sitting here, I realised I was quite lost. I stood. Well, I suppose I should find my way to the nearest police establishment and make my inquiries there, but what questions would I ask? Leaving the little café, I thought I'd begin my interrogation saying that I was in search of a relative, my mother. But how did we get separated? What was her last known address? Oh, dear me, I had better find another way. Oh, but of course, a private detective—but where would I find such a man?

✳ ✳ ✳

"Bow Street," said the hotel concierge at the Mivart where we were staying. "Ask for the Detective Department, miss. You may mention my name, Mr Henry Fielding."

"Oh, very good, sir. I thank you."

"I'll have a coach take you there."

"Very good, Mr Fielding, I would appreciate it. I am new to London, you see."

"Yes, I know."

Dear me, was my prison slang that noticeable? "I beg your pardon, sir?"

"Brighton, perhaps?"

"Oh, indeed, yes, I was there a good many years. How funny it is that we pick up the voice."

"Oh, indeed, miss. I hear very many accents all the day long."

"Oh, yes, I suppose you would. Again, thank you, sir." I took up Hawkeye's leash. "Good day."

I was taken to the Metropolitan Police of London, and after speaking with a rather brusque policeman in regards to my inquiries, I was met with scepticism. I had to quickly assume my impatient, demanding air. I think I frightened him when I dropped Lady Sheffield's name as a close confidant, flashing her card, and insisted upon speaking only with the highest authority in the department.

I was immediately situated in a mahogany waiting parlour of some sort with papers to fill out. After doing so, I noticed three other patrons sitting about. I chose to remain standing, as Hawkeye snuggled deeply into the folds of my skirt, hidden almost. The poor dear's good eye was enfolded in my skirt. "We shan't be much longer, my dear," I said to him. I knew by now he was no doubt very hungry. Not noticing the dog at my side, those sitting about stared at me as if I were quite daft.

It was within the hour that the room was vacated, each man being called and led out of the room by a uniformed policeman. Hopefully, I would be ... the door suddenly opened.

"Miss Wilson, please come this way."

I was led down a very long corridor, my boots thumped the floor in loud and discordant knocks. Finally at its end, I was ushered into a quiet, small room. It smelled of cherry tobacco. I brought my lacy handkerchief to my nose.

"You may take a seat, madam. A detective will be right with you."

I nudged Hawkeye. "Finally."

The door opened, and a very fine looking man stepped in. He was tallish, with a twinge of grey about his temples, cheery bright blue eyes. Reading glasses were atop his head, a pencil in his left hand. "Miss Grace Wilson, I presume, or is it Miss Philips?"

I stood and nodded, I felt my face redden. "My real name is Grace Wilson, sir. I was given the name Philips when put in prison, but for what reason I do not know, sir."

He glanced down at me over his spectacles. "I see." He grasped the doorknob to his office, opened the creaky-hinged door and walked in. "Welcome to Scotland Yard, Miss Wilson. I am Detective Inspector Peter Palgrave," he said over his shoulder.

I followed him in due silence. The room was very austere, with only a few pieces of paper on his desk and his squeaky leather chair. There was another chair situated directly in front of his desk. I sat there. Set on a side table, I noticed a stack of books, the one on top being: *The Murders in the Rue Morgue.* I shuddered.

"Would you care for a glass of water, miss?"

"No, thank you sir, but I am most certain Hawkeye would appreciate a bowl."

He glanced down at the ol' boy and smiled. "Oh, well then, of course." He rummaged about his desk and soon brought out a bowl. I assumed it was for his daily soup.

"Thank you, sir."

He glanced at me with a half-smile and set down the bowl. Rubbing the good side of Hawkeye's head, he smiled. "Hmm, run into a little trouble, I see."

"The trouble being a boot, sir." I said with great indignation. "Indeed, a vile creature of a groom, if there ever was one, I assure you, but it was entirely no fault of Hawkeye's. Why, my feathers ruffle at the very thought." I pursed my lips remembering the whole of it and mighty sorry for the remembrance.

"I see."

He poured Hawkeye fresh water, to the brim.

"There now, drink your heart out my courageous badger boy."

Badger boy? Why, what could he mean by the name?

Hawkeye paused momentarily sniffing the detective's hand.

"He likes you, Inspector Palgrave. And so do I." With a good feeling about this man, I scooted back into my chair, (though hard and bent straight) grateful for finding such an inspector. *Now perhaps we will be able to find Mother, Lord Allenton, Cooke ...*

Detective Palgrave grunted. "Well, I am much relieved for that. He looks like a badger hound. I once owned such a dog. Faithful to the end, so they are."

To the end, indeed. I frowned and sighed deeply. *To what end I am not at all certain.* "He has a great memory, sir. Mr Snivel was the groom who kicked his eye out."

"Oh, dear me, you don't say?"

"Oh, indeed," I huffed. "Hawkeye never forgave him. Traveling by coach to London, Mr Snivel accidentally found our coach and boarded it. Hawkeye challenged him and won."

The detective laughed. "I would have bet on Hawkeye myself."

I smiled. "Indeed, sir."

"When did you board the coach to London and from where, Miss Wilson?"

I shook my head in thought. "Sir, I am not at all sure which village we were in to be exact." I tried to think back to where I stayed the night, the name of the inn. "I think I have the notice here in my purse." I searched through my little draw-string purse, but came up with nothing. "Let me think." I glanced up at the ceiling in thought and noticed a spider web dangling from one corner of the ceiling to the other and wondered where "it" was hiding. "The George, sir, I remember it now. Quite a nice room with a lovely view of the town, Inspector."

"And that is where Mr Snivel kicked Hawkeye?"

"Oh, no, sir, Mr Snivel kicked Hawkeye at Peabury."

"Peabury? The Peabury outside Brighton? Lord Sheffield's Peabury?"

"The very one, sir." I smiled, thankful the inspector was cognizant of such a place, perhaps adding authenticity to my explanation."

"You said Mr Snivel was the groom, if I am not mistaken."

"Head groom, sir, but certainly had no *head* for animals. Why, my very first day there I was nicknamed the animal girl."

"Oh, animal girl, indeed, get along well with the animals, do you?"

"I calmed her ladyship's mare, Raven, considerably, sir. Had her eating out of my hand within a blink of an eye, sir."

"Her ladyship or Raven, Miss Wilson?"

"Oh, sir, why Raven, of course."

"And Hawkeye, I might add."

"Yes, inspector." I squirmed in my seat. "You must find me bragging, sir. I do apologise. I had no prior knowledge that I blend so well with the animals. I just talk to them, treat them as equals, give them dignity, curtsey, even."

"Curtsey?" He hemmed. "Did her ladyship curtsey to Raven?"

I smiled with a blush. "Oh, indeed, sir, she did, and mighty thankful for winning back the affections of her horse. His lordship was to do away with her, sir. Oh, I mean the mare, sir, not her ladyship. That's when it all began, sir."

"Go on," he said looking deeply into my eyes. The lone window in the room cast a bright light upon his face. His eyes crinkled, his skin tanned and rumpled with what I imagined sorrowful cases of debauchery, murder, mayhem of all sorts.

"I was assigned to ride with her ladyship since Raven was such a handful. You know his lordship worries about her so. Though I earlier calmed the mare, it was the bit, sir, that riled the mare so. It was harsh and annoying, and without due care, could have easily severed her tongue."

"Ghastly."

I nodded. "In front of her ladyship, I removed the bridle and bit and fitted the mare with a more humane one, nothing to be inserted in her mouth until it healed. I then instructed her ladyship to remove her gloves to let Raven feel her ladyship's kind hand. And in so doing, her ring fell into the glove that she stuffed inside her riding jacket."

I looked into his inquisitive eyes. "Later she discovered she had lost the ring and Mrs Miles, the housekeeper, assumed I stole it."

"Why would Mrs Miles assume such a thing, Miss Wilson?" He glanced down at the papers I had filled out earlier. "Grace Wilson born in London, located to Brighton some twelve odd years ago. Again, I'm curious, why would she assume such a thing from such a refined, educated lady like yourself?"

"Well, sir, that is precisely why I am here." Hawkeye stood and stretched, sniffed the bowl and sat down with a bored yawn. I kissed his muzzle. He probably had to pee.

"I am really not a lady, sir." I pulled out the note from Lady Sheffield along with her card, the roll of money and handed it to him. "I will repay her, sir, every penny, but sir, I had to look presentable, talk properly or no one would have believed me, inspector."

He read her ladyship's note, seeming to study it and then folded it and left it lying on the desk along with her ladyship's personal calling card and the huge roll of money.

"I was accused, sir, of stealing Lady Sheffield's ring by Mrs Miles, because I was imprisoned at Brighton for twelve years for stealing Lady Allenton's ring. I was cleared of all wrongdoing by her ladyship, for she found her ring in her glove.

Then I decided it was time for me to move on. I left and again began my search for my mother and Lord Allenton ... to clear my name, sir." He sat back in his swivel chair, a squeaky leather chair with well-worn, shiny oak arms. His hands were clasped. I noticed they were hands of someone who washed them frequently. His nails were clean and well-trimmed. "I was wrongly accused of stealing Lady Allenton's ring."

"Along with Lady Sheffield's ring then?"

"Yes, that's it precisely. Well, sir the *first* accusation was twelve years ago." I went on to explain the kind Lord Allenton who bought my daisies, my mother, Mr Buffle, Mr Cooke, and so forth, indeed, everything leading up to leaving Peabury ... everything.

"This constable, Mr O'Malacy, who arrested you and Lord Allenton, how did you come to learn of his name?"

I closed my eyes and tried to remember. "As he was pulling me down the alley by my braids, and by Lord Allenton's neck, his lordship demanded to know his name. The policeman guffawed at such a request. 'Indeed, you old fool, remember it well,' he bowed in mockery, 'it's Mr O'Malacy to you, me lardship.' And with that, he cruelly pushed him into a pile of house slop. I wrenched myself free and helped his lordship to his feet, but the old soul was shaking so, bleeding from his scrapes ..." I dabbed my eyes. "I have since been very frightened of the police, sir."

Inspector Palgrave maintained a stoic face. I could not exactly read what he was thinking, no doubt trying to think of some excuse for O'Malacy's bad conduct. I assumed all policemen stuck together like glue.

"We were taken to a red brick building somewhere near the Thames, I think. It was a cold and blustery afternoon by then. I could hear the splash of the river, the horns; felt the damp, chilly winds. While there, they asked me my name, my age, where I lived. That's when they must have written down Anne Philips and put down the wrong date of my birth, apparently. I didn't know exactly where I lived, and Mr O'Malacy, who was guard over us shrugged. 'No matter, river rats don't have homes.'

"When his lordship began to protest, he was knocked entirely off his feet. I turned my head, fearful of witnessing further abuse. When they chained me up with another person, I called back to his lordship promising to come for him as soon as I was free. O'Malacy slapped his thigh. "You'll be an old hag by then.""

The inspector glanced down at his notes. "Who is this Mary Agnes Bennett, Miss Wilson?"

"We were chained together for what seemed months, sir. I learned her ways quickly. Once I have cleared my reputation, I will find her as well. I love her, sir, almost as much as Mama. Mary Agnes protected me, taught me how to survive; covered me with her body so that the guards wouldn't touch me."

"What did she do to be put in prison?"

"Oh, I think more than she cared to share with me, sir. For one, she was there when I was thrown in and was there when I left."

"Where on earth did you learn to speak with such a refined tongue, then?"

"Mama repaired books from the lending library, sir. She would read to me at night by the candle. She taught me to write, to speak properly. She taught me to speak ignorant as well."

"Ignorant? Why was that, Miss Wilson?"

"If you wear rags you must speak accordingly, sir. Mama said our kind should not trust people who speak well. She was right, for I learned that in prison and at Peabury." I smiled. "But, animals do not discriminate so violently, they only respond to kind words, kind touches."

He smiled. "Indeed, Miss Wilson." He glanced down at Hawkeye. "There is a side yard you make take the ol' boy. I have a few things to sort out while you are gone, that is, if you don't mind."

"Oh, I do not mind at all, Inspector Palgrave, not at all." I stood. Hawkeye hurried toward the door, pulling me along. "You're correct, sir," I nodded. "Mr Hawkeye has some business to do."

Chapter 8 – Searching London Streets

"This way, Miss Wilson."

I followed Inspector Palgrave out of his office and to the side yard and unleashed Hawkeye and watched him run and stretch. Sniffing this and that, he did his business. There was a lovely garden a few yards from where we were, and I decided to stroll through it. We were alone, the day sky was clear, the trees full and leafy with green, thick and waxy. A few sparrows darted about, eyeing us with trepid little jerks of their heads. I half-listened to the familiar clop of horses just over the wall from us, the grind of leather, the jingle of their bells, a shout, a cough …"

"There you are, Miss Wilson," said the inspector.

Hawkeye came running toward him with his tail wagging as if he was his long lost friend.

"Oh, sir, I am so happy Hawkeye has taken to you."

He stooped and jovially petted his head. "Why is that, Miss Wilson?"

"It means you are a man of integrity, sir."

His brows furrowed at my estimation, I assumed. "I wouldn't be in Scotland Yard, miss, if I were any other sort of man."

I glanced out over the flower garden with a weary sigh. "Indeed, sir. Some of *your sort* are not though, not at all with integrity, sir. Sorry to say."

"Follow me, Miss Wilson. I have a few more questions to ask of you."

After a few steps, he asked, "so, your mother taught you to read and write?"

"Yes, sir," I smiled at the recollection.

"She was an educated woman, then. How could that be?" He walked to the window and stared out at nothing. "I mean, living in squalor, in an alley, of all places?"

"Sir, I do not remember living in squalor. Mama always made me sweep. "

"How was it she was educated?"

I thought for a moment, not really sure. "Perhaps she was

a governess, a lady's maid, a teacher. I, I really do not know, sir. Oh, if we could only find my little house in the alley, all of this would surely make sense."

"There are many alleys in London, Miss Wilson."

"It was not far from Lord Allenton's townhouse, sir. That much I remember. I carried her ladyship's shoes ... I walked down the alley to the gate. I got lost one evening when the fog moved in."

"When Mr Cooke slipped and fell? You retrieved the ring, as I recall."

"Yes, that's it exactly."

"What did it look like, Miss Wilson."

"Oh, sir, it was really quite spectacular. It was a huge blue-white diamond sparkling in a crown of silver filigree, the likes of which I have never seen before."

"Very much like Lady Sheffield's?"

"Oh, sir, I do not know. I have never seen her ladyship's ring."

He nodded. "Mr Cooke said the ring belonged to his mother, is that right?"

"His mother? No, sir, only that it was in his family for many years. Yes, sir, those were his very words, and I believed him ... then."

"Then and not now?"

"I am not at all sure anymore, sir. When I presented the ring to O'Malacy, his Lordship gasped saying it was his wife's and that it had been stolen."

"What happened to the ring again, if I may? My memory is so short, you see."

"Oh, that is no worry, sir. I've not forgotten a thing."

"Except where you live."

I glanced at the inspector with a sigh. "That's right, sir."

"Again, what happened to the ring?"

I handed it to Mr O'Malacy as proof of my story."

"What did he do with it, Miss Wilson?"

"O'Malacy gaped at such a sparkly beauty. He then looked at me saying, 'Well well, now, we know who stole it.' He then huffed greatly and stuck it in his purse."

"Describe the purse."

I thought for a moment. "It was dark in the ally, sir. I think it was a small black leather one, with a silver clasp. It hung diagonally across his uniform and was buckled to his waist-cinch. Very near his baton."

"The time of day, again, was in the morning?"

"No, sir, late evening, and it was turning very cold by the hour. I only had my check apron for warmth."

"How did you know it was *late* evening? Did you hear the chimes of the town clock, perhaps?"

"The clock? Oh, sir, indeed I did, now that you mention it. Mama always insisted on being home before the tenth gong. She would say, 'Poppy, you must listen for the clock, and be home before ten.' "

"Poppy?"

"The name was given to me because of my red hair, sir, but usually Mama called me Grace." I smiled at the recollection, "I was quite the sprite back then, sir. Always giggling, springing about like a poppy flower selling my bunch of flowers; helping mama sweep her corner."

"Her corner, Miss Wilson? Where might that be?"

"The one ... just below Tuppence Lane." In shocked disbelief, I glanced up at the inspector. "Why, sir, Tuppence just rolled off my tongue. You have found it."

He smiled. "Well, not just yet, Miss Wilson. We have not yet found your little home in the alley, but perhaps."

I stood, much excited. Hawkeye sprung from his sleep, glancing around excitedly, growling.

"Calm yourself, ol' boy," said the inspector. "Your mistress is in very good hands."

"Oh, indeed, sir. Oh, how grateful I am to you." I hugged Hawkeye. "To think, we are finally on our way to finding Mama." I bowed my head and wept. "I cannot believe such a thing. I have you to thank." I paced about the room. "Well, I must leave you to your work, sir. I assume you are very busy, but I want to help. What if Hawkeye and I did a little searching of our own?"

"I think it wiser if I accompanied you, Miss Wilson." He glanced at the papers on his desk. "You are staying at the Mivart Hotel? Yes? Well, I will see you there in the lobby at eleven, sharp tomorrow morning, if that, of course, suits you?"

"Oh, indeed, sir." I leashed Hawkeye and bid the inspector a very good afternoon.

"Allow me, Miss Wilson to hail a coach. It will be dark very soon."

"Thank you, sir ... for treating me like a lady." I glanced out the window. "I do hope it is not against the law to impersonate one."

* * *

The very next morning as the Inspector and I sat in the Twinings' Tea Shop, I explained a little of my past. "Lord Allenton always bought my daisies even though he had his own garden."

"Have you met his sons? I've learned he has two."

"Not his firstborn, inspector, but his second, Dr Moore. He is now a very respectable physician."

"Oh, yes. He was the one who sent money to his mother, in America, is it?"

"I think so, sir. That is what he told me."

"And you believed him, I presume."

I glanced at his serious, inspector's face and nodded. "Well, he attends Lady Sheffield. He is her nephew, sir."

"*Her* nephew? By which relative."

Her ladyship's sister is Lady Allenton, so I was told. And her son, Dr Patrick Moore, was attending Cambridge when news came of his father's disappearance. They kept the news that his father began to wander aimlessly. They only told him of his father's disappearance when he returned from school. They had given up all hope of finding the elder gentleman thinking he fell into the Thames."

"Did you mention to Dr Moore or any other person what you witnessed regarding Lord Allenton being tied up, beaten, and taken to jail?"

"No, sir. I felt it would only add misery to their lives. They all seem very well adjusted at his absence – except of course, the younger, Dr Moore. He was still very saddened at the loss of his father. Besides all that, sir, who would believe me, an ex-prisoner? No, I have remained quiet as a mouse, until of course, seeking you out."

"Very good, Miss Wilson. I would wish it of you to maintain your silence a little while longer. It will prove to be invaluable to my investigation."

"Oh, indeed, inspector." My chest swelled with pride. "I will remain silent as a stone, I promise, sir."

"Very well, then."

After finishing our tea, we boarded a coach for hire. I settled back in my seat and watched as we traversed along Bishopsgate Street, turning up Threadneedle Street, past the impressive Bank of England, on toward the Thames. I glanced up each and every alley.

"Anything look familiar, Miss Wilson?"

"Not yet, inspector, but it has been over twelve years now. Do you suppose they closed the alley or named it something?" I had twisted my lovely lace handkerchief into knots.

"We'll see soon enough, Miss Wilson, but do be mindful, London's street keepers are doing a much better job than in the past."

"At sweeping, sir?"

He nodded. "Her Majesty is out touring today, a rare occasion. She is fond of riding past Prince Albert's Great Exhibition ... the crystal palace."

"How very nice." I glanced out the window not knowing what he was speaking of. How could anyone build a house out of crystal anyway? "I have long been absent from England's progress these many years, sir. I do apologise for my ignorance regarding such matters."

"Oh, what do we commoners know anyway? I wouldn't put too much into your absence or lack thereof. Our opinions count very little, it seems."

"I really cannot say, inspector, but I suppose my opinion isn't worth a penny."

"Perhaps."

"Oh, look there, The Red Teapot, and there," I pointed excitedly, "Hanny's Silver Shoppe. Oh, stop, stop this instant, we are very close."

Immediately the coach veered to the side curb and stopped at the request of Inspector Palgrave. Hawkeye jumped out first. I took in a great breath and pointed up the street. "That way, sir."

Hawkeye stopped to sniff every pole, shop stoop, and wet mark to the consternation of the inspector. "Sorry, sir."

He nodded. "Anything more looking familiar, Miss Wilson?"

We continued down Tuppence Lane, squinting in the bright morning light. Ladies and gentlemen hem-hawed around us; little children scurried about crying and fussing at one thing or the other.

"Some things look familiar, sir." I stopped at the corner crossing that met an alley. "Which way is the Thames?"

"That way," pointed the inspector.

"Let us move on to The Red Teapot." We hurried forth. I nearly tripped over Hawkeye who had stopped directly in my path to sniff. "Go on now, ol' boy." Finally jostling to get my bearings, I looked up at the shop's name. We stopped directly in front of The Red Teapot. "Sir, it looks the very same, so it does."

"Frequented it a great deal?"

"I hand-carried bundles of their linens ... after I ironed them, sir. Mama tied theirs with red ribbon, Hanny's was blue ..."

Palgrave held the door. Of course Hawkeye was the first in, sniffing here and there. Once inside, I recollected everything instantly—the same small room, warmth, the smell of iced-cakes, mocha coffee brewing. The walls were festooned with Albert and Victoria, silver teaspoons set stacked upon one another on the side-board. A warm fire in the hearth with its cavernous stone walls burnt, blackened, and caked with char centuries old was surrounded by white wicker furniture. A cheery window framed with lovely ivory lace curtains dressed the shop.

"Yes, inspector, the very place." I nodded, gleeful for the recollection. Walking up to the counter, I glanced around to where the linens used to be stacked, neatly folded. I pointed with a smile. "Ah, the very place, sir."

"May I help you, madam?" said a young girl wearing a crisp white frilly apron about her. Her hair pulled up neatly tucked beneath her white cap, her red cheeks plump and shiny.

I took hold of her apron and admired its starched whiteness, ironed properly. "Oh, perhaps you can, miss. I was wondering, who does your laundry?"

She looked at me as if I had lost my mind. Indeed, why would a lady of such refinement ask such a question? "Oh, madam, our laundry is done by a washerwoman ..."

"Oh, yes," I smiled broadly, "do go on. Do you know where she lives? What is her name?"

The inspector took my elbow. "Miss Wilson," he whispered discreetly, "perhaps we should sit and take tea first. Let *me* do the questioning, if you please."

"Oh," I glanced around. The other patrons were staring at us and whispering. "Why, indeed, sir."

We were situated at the window, Hawkeye at my feet. "I beg your pardon, Inspector Palgrave. I was just ..."

"Leave the questioning to me, Miss Wilson."

I felt my face redden again.

"I know this is all very vexing and you want to find your mother. Believe me, I do understand."

"Yes, sir, I know you do."

When the young girl came to take our order, she stood a little distance, closer to Inspector Palgrave. "Sir, what may I bring you?"

"We'll have Earl Grey and the usual scones—butter and jam. That will be all."

"Indeed, sir." The young girl smiled at him and ignored me completely.

"Well, I must have seemed quite the odd one, didn't I?"

He shook his head. "No, Miss Wilson, you're not odd in the least—perhaps a little overly excited."

When the girl brought her tray with the teapot and scones to us, Inspector Palgrave hemmed, "I say, miss, I am Inspector Detective Palgrave, Scotland Yard ..."

Her bright blue eyes grew wide. She set the pot down. "Oh, indeed, sir."

"I was wondering, if you don't mind telling, who do you employ to launder your linens? We cannot help but notice how nicely they are done up."

She smiled. "Just recently, by several months, sir, my father has employed a Mrs Brown."

"And where might we find this Mrs Brown?"

"That sir, I am not familiar." She set down the butter, jam, and scones. "Clotted cream?"

"Oh, indeed."

She smiled again. "I will ask my father."

The lovely little tea-girl returned within a very few minutes. "Father does not know where exactly Mrs Brown lives, sir. Sorry to say, but she takes the soiled things every night, promptly at ten o'clock in the evening."

"I see. Well, thank you. What time do you close?"

"Nine o'clock, sir."

Oh, who might this Mrs Brown be? Would she know my mother? I could feel my little heart pound. "Oh, inspector, I could certainly come back here tonight."

"No, Miss Wilson. I would rather you leave this investigation to me. It would not be proper for a lady to be out without a chaperone. Besides, it would be much too dangerous."

I dropped my head. "Oh, indeed, sir."

"Well," he sipped the last of his tea, "come now, we must be on our way."

Now standing just outside the little tea room, I squinted and gestured toward an opening between the buildings. "Let us go down this little way."

"Looks familiar docs it?"

I sniffed the air. "No, inspector, no it really does not look ... wait," I paused turning the corner, "come, perhaps this is the way, sir." We walked a little distance farther and then I spied the gate.

"Oh, here we are, sir." I pointed in excitement. "There it is." Hawkeye ran alongside me as we approached what I thought was the red brick mansion of Lord Allenton's. Now stopped, we gazed at the house. "Well, it looks to be the very one, sir. And much repaired from the last time I stood here. Before there were leaves cluttered about the carriage-porch, the basement window was broken. I swept that very porch fearing his lordship would be upset to return home and find such a mess."

"Indeed," he said, nodding thoughtfully.

As we approached the old oaken door, I pointed to the once shiny ornament on its front. "The very same knocker, sir, but back then, I was much too small to reach the bell-pull and used a broom to lift the brass lion knocker."

"And Mr Buffle scolded you when he found you wandering about the house?"

"Oh, sir, I wasn't wandering about at all. I had just entered when a gust of wind slammed the door behind me. He suddenly appeared."

The inspector nodded and took hold of the knocker and clanged it several times. No one came to the door.

I offered a bit of encouragement, "It may be unlocked, sir ..."

He stiffened and gave me a sour look. "Indeed not, Miss Wilson." He clanged the knocker a few times more and then walked back down the stairs glancing about. Neighbourhood dogs growled and barked, but none brave enough to challenge Hawkeye, I supposed. I followed the inspector to the back of the house.

"There sir, is the stable." Standing in front of the garden gate, I anxiously glanced up the alley that led in from the opposite direction—that was the way home. I reflected back to the day I hurried from our little alley home with the ring in my apron pocket. So anxious to find Mr Cooke, but instead found the dear Lord Allenton. "That is the way to my little alley home, sir." I pointed.

We walked up the ally for a little distance when Palgrave stopped and looked back at the Great House. I supposed a better view of the stables and garden from this perspective.

"Remain here, Miss Wilson, I will be only a moment."

I watched the inspector walk toward the House. Hawkeye sniffed the air, whined, and then nudged my leg. "Yes, he's a fine policeman, ol' boy. We were lucky to have found him, and I do believe he finds my story truthful."

I turned and glanced once more to the stables. Curiosity

tugged at me. Dare I go back into that dreadful place where his Lordship sat tied up and gagged? Why not, I asked. Inspector Palgrave is only a scream away.

"Come Hawkeye, you'll protect me."

"Stay where you are, Miss Wilson," Palgrave called back over his shoulder.

"Oh, indeed, sir." I frowned at Hawkeye with a scold. "You must not tempt me so."

Within a few minutes, we spied the inspector coming from around the other side of the house. Glancing into the windows, he shook his head. There did not seem to be anyone there. Surely a few servants would be on hand, but I was wrong, apparently.

"Miss Wilson, show me where Constable O'Malacy found you and his lordship."

"Right this way, sir."

I took him to the side of the stables where there used to be the apple orchard, the thorny fruit bushes. Glancing at the side of the barn, I shook my head. "Oh, it looks to have been boarded up, sir." I inspected the side of the barn. "You see here," I pointed, "someone has boarded it up completely, hiding evidence no doubt. Shall we go inside? I will show you the stairs."

"That will not be necessary." He stood for a moment studying the stables, the boarded up side of the barn, the orchard and then he turned to me. "O'Malacy dragged you and his lordship up this alley?"

"Yes, sir."

"Do you remember how long it took you to reach the police department from this point?"

I thought for a second. "No, not exactly, but if you wish we could walk it now. It was just that way."

"Well, that won't be necessary. I have a good idea where he took you both."

"May we now go in search of my mother?"

With a stern look, he nodded and glanced once more at the barn. "Come along, then."

We walked up the alley toward my little home, the three of us. It looked very much the same in many ways. Laundry hung out the windows, grey and dingy. Pools of stench lay seeping into the cracks of the cobbles beneath the soles of my boots. The smell of rottenness was trapped between the dark red brick buildings that leaned toward one another, nearly touching from one side to the other.

"Up just a ways, sir, I believe, but this part does not look familiar." I sniffed the air. "It smells much more putrid."

"Indeed, Miss Wilson, you've been gone a long time."

Coming to the steps that led down to a warped and cracked door, I stopped. "This is the place, I am sure of it." The one lone window had no candle in it, only a hardened snub of soured yellow wax stuck hard to the sill. Taking the inspector's arm, I took in a great breath and closed my eyes. "Oh, sir, I cannot look. I am afraid to knock upon that door. It looks so small and decrepit. I think no one lives there anymore."

"Stay where you are, Miss Wilson. I will see for myself. You may take Hawkeye and move on a little distance, if you wish it."

"No, we'll remain here."

I could not bear to look. Think of the disappointment. I heard the tap, the creak of the door's opening. I held my breath.

"I am Inspector Detective Palgrave, Scotland Yard ..."

I opened my eyes and took a few steps closer. There stood an old woman, with grey, frizzy hair. Frail and worn thin, I swallowed hard. *Oh, my, that is not Mama.*

Inspector Palgrave gestured for me. "Miss Wilson, please come."

I smiled at the frail creature standing in the doorway. "Good afternoon, ma'am." I nodded.

"If you are not Mrs Wilson, might you know where she has gone?" asked the inspector. "Do you mind if we come in?"

I did not see the need to enter the old woman's place, but Hawkeye did.

She chuckled as he hurriedly brushed past her, his tail wagging. "Come, sir, but ye won't find nothing.' When I moved here, there were lots o' children with their Ma and Pa, and books stacked everywhere. Me thinks they even burnt some in the pit to stay warm."

I glanced around at the hearth, it of course was the very same, chips and missing bricks—the lone window, still filthy with grime of one sort or the other. No, there was nothing here to remind me of Mama but the walls.

"Has anyone else inquired about Mrs Wilson?"

"Oh, but a few years ago a man came to call."

"Did he leave his card, his name? Can you recall anything at all?"

"No, and he didn't leave no card."

"O'Malacy?" I asked.

Her face contorted in a question mark. "Hmm, no."

"A Mr Cooke?" said the inspector.

"I don't recall his name being Cooke, sir."

"Very well, then, madam we'll be on our way."

She closed the door quietly at our backs. We stood for a little time just looking up and down the alley.

"I am truly sorry you didn't find your mother, Miss Wilson, but we're not done yet."

Just as we were beginning to walk away, the door opened, and the old woman shuffled out. "Inspector, there is someone who might know of this Mrs Wilson."

"Indeed."

She pointed. "Up that way, 'round the corner you'll find the lending library. Somebody from there left an armload of books on me step. Took weeks to find out who did such a thing."

"Oh, indeed, Inspector Palgrave, Mama used to mend them for the library. I had nearly forgotten."

The old woman's eyes widened. "Your mama?"

"We used to live here, ma'am."

The inspector touched his hat. "Thank you, ma'am, we'll be on our way." We found the lending library. The very same building I had gone to as a child. Nothing seemed to have changed. The same shelves of books, and the same smell of worn paper and glue. Book carts piled high, a counter with a portly be-speckled gentleman sitting behind it.

In a low tone, he smiled up at us. "May I be of service, sir?"

The inspector took out his card and handed it up to him. "Who repairs your books, sir?"

The librarian took the card and stood. "Oh, Inspector Palgrave, we send everything out." He glanced at me. "We used to bind and repair them here, but now it's cheaper to send them to Williams Book Shoppe. Might you need one repaired, sir? I would be happy to add it to our next shipment. Mr Williams comes daily to the library."

"Oh, no, that will not be necessary, Mr ?"

"Merriweather, Inspector Palgrave. I am senior librarian here, have been for several years now." He removed his spectacles and smiled down at me.

"Do you recall a Mrs Wilson who used to repair books here?"

"Mrs Wilson? He thought for a moment. "No, I do not recall a Mrs Wilson, but it's not my memory, sir. It's that we go through so many. They come and go like the weather, you know. Not dependable in the least."

I hemmed. "Sir, do you remember a little girl, red hair, her name was Poppy?"

"Poppy?" He frowned. "No, the name does not sound familiar." He glanced up at my hair. "Might you be Poppy?"

Just then the frail old lady shuffled in, her cape snuggled about her neck, her finger waving in the air. "I just remembered the name of that gentleman who came calling ... Allen, sir."

The Inspector looked intently at her. "Might you be mistaken, madam? Could it have been an Allenton, perhaps? Lord Allenton?"

She dropped her head in thought, touching her mouth. "Oh, well now, maybe."

"Lord Allenton?" said the librarian, "Why, his lordship has been gone many years now."

"You know him, Mr Merriweather?" asked the inspector.

"Oh, heavens no, not his lordship, only his son, he came in by and by."

"The elder or the younger."

"The earl had only one son, inspector."

Palgrave glanced at me. He still held a face impossible to read. *One son? Why, there were two. Did Palgrave think I made this all up? Oh, dear me, who and what am I to believe? Surely Dr Moore would not have made it up ... not the nephew of Lady Sheffield.*

"Yes, well," said the inspector, "we'll be on our way." He bid his adieus to the librarian, and we escorted the old woman back to her doorstep. We thanked her and moved back down the alley. Hawkeye pranced ahead, pulling at his leash, his tail high in the air.

"I think he needs to be free, sir."

He nodded and watched me unleash Hawkeye for a short jaunt along the alleyway.

"Inspector Palgrave, forgive me, but it seems you must think me a liar. Nothing is making sense." I took in a great breath. "I am even beginning to doubt my own existence." I glanced around. "Am I really here? Could so many people have deceived me?" Taking my handkerchief from my pocket, I dabbed my eyes. "I suppose, sir, you think I have wasted your very valuable time. And for that, I am very sorry. I should continue on by myself. I will get to the bottom of all of this, I assure you."

"Not alone, you won't, Miss Wilson."

"I beg your pardon, sir?"

"I will hail a coach and return you to the Mivart. I have a number of things I will look into, but you must not continue on alone. It just may dampen the investigation."

"Very well, inspector." I called for Hawkeye, and we proceeded back down the alley and past Lord Allenton's townhouse. I stopped to view the basement window. "You see, sir, the window I spoke about that was broken?" I pointed. "His lordship would never have had such a sloppy house. It would have been repaired immediately. I am not so sure Mr Buffle or Mr Cooke were his butlers after all."

"Indeed." He stood glancing around at the house. "Well, Miss Wilson, all of this will take a bit of sorting out."

I knew he didn't believe me. Who would? All the information I had given him thus far was unsupportable. I shook my head and found Hawkeye whining at my feet. "Well, ol' boy did you enjoy your little jaunt?" I leashed him and smiled up at the inspector.

"He's a loyal ol' cur, so he is." He petted Hawkeye's head. "Best to keep him close to your side, Miss Wilson. He'll not let harm come to you."

I felt a chill run up my spine. "Oh, indeed, sir," I paused, "why would you think such a thing, inspector?"

He scoffed. "Oh, pay no heed. It's just my overly-protective nature at work." He looked at me with a tender smile. "I had a daughter near your age," he exhaled, "always better to keep a jaundiced eye about, Miss Wilson. There are always those few who are bent on doing evil."

I nodded. "Thank you, sir." Glancing up at the sky, I felt a twinge of envy. "I never had a father. I would suppose your daughter is very fortunate to have one who cares for her."

"She died, Miss Wilson—last year, in fact."

"Your daughter, sir?"

With a sorrowful nod, he glanced away. The wrinkles on his face held a shadow of terrible pain. "Oh, sir, I am very sorry." It was the way he stared at the ground, his breathing shallow, his lips pursed and I knew not to question him further. My own heart was heavy—how terribly sad I was for him. I had rather suspected all along that he had thought of me as a defenceless young woman, and had become protective in a fatherly sort of way. If he only knew ... well, of course he knew of my prior life in prison and the conditions I endured as a child growing up in such confusion and riotousness. And I rather felt ashamed being sheltered by him now. I could certainly manage on my own.

"Inspector, here I am in these lovely clothes, dressed fine as any lady, and yet customs forbid me to go out without a man on my arm, for fear of impropriety. Before wearing these beautiful clothes, I would meander just about anywhere in any city in my servant's attire. Indeed, I have slept off the road many, many nights, alone. Smart enough to hide from highwaymen. I built my fires with discretion, slept with no fear, but now, now being dressed in these elegant fineries I am the target of pickpockets, thieves and the worst sort. Sir, I wonder at the idea of having money."

I drew the strings to my purse a little tighter. "Oh, indeed, having money has its rewards, sir." I smiled. "Dining just last evening at a fine table, I admired the Limoges china, dainty tea-cups, silver settings, cloth napkins, and there sitting in the centre of it all, a cut-glass bowl full of roses of pinks, reds, whites—their fragrance was almost overwhelming.

"It brought back memories of my treks along the highway where I had an abundance of fragrant wildflowers just as beauti-ful, and they weren't meant to live only a day in a bowl of smelly water. I drank from a well-worn tin cup, and the water tasted just as sweet as that poured for me into fine crystal. The leaves scat-tered before me seemed just as lovely as the superb Irish linen my plate sat upon. Money? Is it all so necessary to have such a great abundance when one must be suspicious of all those around you—to live in fear of being robbed and killed for the prestige of flaunting the excesses?"

He sighed, a weariness etched deep in his furrowed brow. "Indeed, but some must steal in order to eat, to feed their fam-ilies. And, yes, some simply steal for the thrill of taking what is not theirs."

I nodded. "Indeed, sir. The morals and manners of the class-es have often confused me. Well, for my part, I was well-off being poor and simple. When I told Lady Sheffield that I was leaving for London in the morning, she must have snuck that huge sum of money into my purse." I gave him a weary glance. "I think, sir, I was happier without such a sum in my purse."

"Oh, perhaps so, Miss Wilson, but then you wouldn't have come this far, would you? You yourself told me how one judges others by their clothes, their speech, their manner. If no one in your family had money, your mother would not have been able to learn to speak properly ... to teach you, as well. So, money has its disadvantages, but along with it comes prudence, fair-minded-ness, and thoughtfulness. Do not be so quick to judge those who are *more* fortunate than you."

I nodded. *He was right in one aspect, Lady Sheffield was an exception, Dr Moore the other.*

"And this Lady Sheffield must have thought very highly of

you to have given you such a sum."

"Indeed, sir, and I aim to repay her. I have a mind to return to Peabury tomorrow, and if allowed, I'll work there until I've repaid what she's given me."

"Well, now, that is very high-minded of you, Miss Wilson, but it may offend her ladyship. After all, it was a gift."

I glanced up at the inspector's serious face. I felt my shoulders shrug, felt my lips purse. "Oh, sir, I have never been given anything of such magnitude before in my entire life. I do not know how to take it without guilt." My lip began to quiver. "How do I rid the feeling of unworthiness, sir?"

"Well, have you not read: *'It is more blessed to give than to receive,'* [5] Miss Wilson? Surely you do not want to take that goodness from her."

My eyes widened. "Oh, no, sir, of course not, but what am I to do?"

"Well, perhaps send her a note with gracious words of gratitude. Explain what you have done thus far in your search for your mother." He paused in thought. "Well, perhaps not everything you've done thus far. I mean to say, do not mention that you've sought me out. Just briefly say you have not yet found your mother. That should do."

I nodded, but my heart was still heavy. "Or I could pay her a visit in person." I smiled feeling very relieved. "Indeed, I shall leave in the morning then."

"Well, I really don't think that is such a good idea, Miss Wilson. We still have much to accomplish here."

"You know as much as I do now, sir." Displeased with myself, I had nothing more to give him. "Indeed, dead ends at every door. It is as if someone had come before us and erased all traces of my existence and his lordship's." I turned to the kind gentleman inspector. "Sir, you have been more than kind helping me. It seems you have become another whom I cannot repay." I dropped my head into my hands. "All of this has become too sordid and confusing for me—vexing and trying. My head aches at all the trouble I have put you through, all for nought."

"Vexing and trying, that is true, my dear Miss Wilson, but I have been at Scotland Yard for many years now, and if I allowed myself to think that way then the evil doers would thrive. I am not about to let that happen. I assure you I will get to the bottom of this. The devils amongst us must be met with a steel fist."

---

5. The Bible, Acts 20:35.

"Indeed, sir." But I knew I was not the steel fist, nor wished to be anything of the sort. Now I just wanted to be on my way, away from this busy city with its turmoil and deceptions. I must find my own peace and repay my debt in some acceptable way to her ladyship.

He kindly put his hand on my shoulder. "Miss Wilson, perhaps some time away would soothe your troubled thoughts."

I must have lit up like a torch. "Oh, thank you, sir. I think I shall. Do forgive me, for leaving you so soon."

"Leave you must, then, Miss Wilson. I sometimes forget how gentle spirits work." He smiled and took from his vest pocket his card. "Take this Miss Wilson, and don't hesitate to use my name, if such a need arises."

I took his card. "Oh, sir, thank you, but I do not think I shall encounter any such obstacle in my travels to warrant ..."

"Do as I say, Miss Wilson."

I wanted to say: *Yes Father, but held my tongue.* "Yes, sir."

"Very good, now I will hail a coach for you." He patted Hawkeye on the head and whispered, "Watch over her ol' boy."

"I shall keep in touch, sir. I promise." I boarded the coach, snuggled Hawkeye at my feet and waved. "Good-day, sir."

Sitting back, I heard the coachman click-whistle to the horses, felt the lurch as we veered out into the busy London street, clopping and edging toward the destination of my hotel—Grosvenor Square. I could still see Inspector Palgrave standing at the curb watching after my coach. I dabbed my eyes and smiled. *I have met a friend in London I shall not soon forget.*

Ambling along, I listened to the hooves clop on the rounded little cobble-stones and found it oddly soothing, the squeak and hustle of the coach put me in mind of the ride I took to the prison many years ago. It struck me odd that I had most recently ridden in a coach more times in two days than I had ever ridden in my entire life.

The passing air smelled of horse dung. A pleasing scent nonetheless, so I found it. A lady and gentleman sat on the forward seat. The lady's hands were folded neatly on her lap, her parasol at her side. Her lovely day frock had tiny red roses embroidered on the skirt. Lovely idea, I thought. Gazing out the window, I watched an old woman, stooped and very tired looking stop and glance up the street before crossing. She looked familiar, but who could look so familiar to me? I do not know anyone here.

"Dear me, it is Mary Agnes Bennett." *Oh, I am sure of it.*

"Please, stop. I must get off here."

The coachman eventually found a place and stopped. I hurried down from the steps, and holding my hat with one hand and Hawkeye's leash with the other, rushed back in the direction where I last saw her. Hurrying through the crowded street, I searched in vain for the red-scarfed old woman. "Oh, don't tell me I have found nothing again." Standing at the corner, I squinted into the early evening sun. "Oh, in which direction might she have gone?" Hawkeye whined. "Oh, I know you want to run." Looking across the busy street, I noticed a bit of green with trees and shrubs. "Come along then, I'll set you free there."

We crossed the street and came into a lovely garden. Sparrows flitted about a smallish pond. The pebbly path was partially leaf-covered; an old horseshoe lay atop a pile of stones. I unleashed Hawkeye with the promise he would not venture far. Turning back to find the bench, I noticed the old woman with a red scarf sitting with her back to me. I approached slowly and sat.

Glancing now at her profile, I was sure of it. "Mary Agnes?"

Startled, she stared back at me clutching her bundle to her chest. "Who are you?"

"Mary Agnes, I am Poppy." I took her shrivelled hand. "Oh, I cannot tell you how happy I am that I have found you."

She withdrew her hand. "You cannot be Poppy." She looked me up and down and then as if discovering a shiny new gold coin, she laughed, "Holy fish, it be you."

"Oh, yes, indeed, it is."

People walking the path stared at me as if I were quite mad, such a fine lady hugging a filthy beggar. I cared not what anyone should think. I was not a fine lady anyway, and I didn't care one philip if I ever became one.

"Oh, Mary Agnes, when did you get set free?"

"About a week after ye left."

"And where have you sheltered?"

"Oh, here and there along the way." She gestured toward an old dilapidated building sitting off in front of us built partway under a bridge. "I'll find my place there tonight."

"Well, it looks quite nice from here."

"We wait 'til dark, you know."

"Oh, yes, I know. I've hidden in them many times on my way back here."

She nodded.

"When I left Brighton, Mary Agnes, I would have counted such a building a great find."

She glanced down at Hawkeye. "That be your hound?"

"It is. His name is Hawkeye." At the mention of his name, Hawk hurried to my side, wiggling. He sniffed Mary Agnes forcing his way between us. "He's my protector, you see."

"Brave little beast." She patted his head with a respectful nod.

"Mary Agnes, would you allow me to give you a little money?" I explained I had come into a tidy sum, where I was staying, and why I returned to London.

"Oh, no, my dear Poppy." She looked at me with a frown. "What would I do with money?"

I smiled. "Well, for one you could take a room, have a quiet bath, change into warmer clothes; have a fire built for you."

She scoffed. "Oh, silly dream girl." She hugged me. "You've always been a dreamer. No, I won't take nothing from you, my dear. I am quite happy to be penniless and free." She glanced up with a proud look. "No worries, I'll find my way."

"Oh, indeed, until "they" need someone to throw in jail. Please understand, Mary Agnes, wearing respectable clothes protects you from suspicion. Won't you allow me to help you? You helped me survive for many years. I would not have lived if it weren't for you."

She seemed to twinge at the truth of that recollection, I was very sure of it.

"I am speaking the truth, and you know it. You must allow me to repay your kindness. It would do my heart much good." I glanced down at the top of Hawkeye's little head. With a deep sigh, I went on, "I have met with nothing but walls since coming here, Mary Agnes. I did not find my mother, I did not find his lordship, but I did find the alley and where I lived, but an old lady lives there now, and she knew nothing of Mama."

She nodded. "Oh, I remember your story, Poppy. Years ago I would've knowed what happened. I knowed the thieves then, but now I knowed nothing and nobody." She gave a bleak gaze to the building she would soon make home. "Been away too long, it seems."

I took her hand. "Then come with me now. We'll buy you some very respectable things to wear." I gently lifted her skirt and exposed her well-worn shoes. "Just look at your boots, Mary Agnes."

One toe stuck out through the well-worn tip of her boot. Wiggling it, we both cackled like mirthful night hags.

I stood. "Come, you will eat with me tonight and stay with

me for a few days until I find a nice place for you to live."

"Oh, Poppy, maybe some boots, but they wouldn't allow me in a fancy hotel, I am sure of it."

"Allow me to first dress you proper, Mary Agnes. We'll pretend you're my maid. You'll not have to say a word. Tomorrow we'll take a train to a lovely town called Croydon. Mr Littlejohn from my hotel spoke fondly of the town. He said I'd find a proper little cottage for settling there, with a garden, a cow, some chickens ..."

Dropping her head into her hands, she cried. "Oh, Poppy girl, you canno afford a place to live for me."

I opened my little purse, glanced around to make sure no one was looking and withdrew the money. "I have enough here to buy a lovely little cottage Mary Agnes, and I will."

She took my hand. "Oh, I canno believe such a thing, Poppy. I canno." She crossed herself. "Oh, thanks be to God my dear angel." She looked down into my little purse and took my hand with a firm grip. "But Poppy, where'd ya be getting' such a sum? You no thief, I knowed that much."

"Then come with me, and I will tell you."

* * *

The very next day Mary Agnes and I stepped off the train near Croydon, about ten miles south of London. Walking into town, we noticed the fieldstone fences, four feet high, at least. Tall green grasses beyond, and beyond that a little silvery river curled in and about meadow lands stretching out far west. The sun was now atop our heads, and a warm breeze flittered about our bonnets. Spotted brown and white cows meandered near the river, ankle deep in grass they grazed, their bellies round and plump.

"This looks to be a fine place to live, Mary Agnes. If anyone should ask, I am your niece." I glanced down at Hawkeye, he was anxious to run. His bandages were beginning to unravel again. "I think he has healed enough." Together we carefully removed them as he squirmed, though quite obedient.

"Aye, he's good as new," said Mary Agnes. "He's eye wrinkled and raggedy, but dry."

Smiling, I patted his head. "Go now you little monster and run."

There we had found a sweet little cottage, well afforded,

with a fine kitchen, well-swept and cared for. The white-washed walls were adorned with a few pictures, a rarity I must say. The hearth was abundant and still held a fine old iron stew pot hanging to the side. There were two very good out-buildings and easy pathways to the river—a nice plot for a good garden and close to the door.

"What have you to say, Mary Agnes. Will this do?"

She walked around inside, her mouth gaping. "I have never lived in such beauty me whole life, Poppy, in me whole life. But what would her ladyship have to say? How can ye pay her back?"

I put my arms around her frail little shoulders. "Do not worry, Mary Agnes. I will find a way." I hugged her. "Very well, then, it is settled. I will purchase this lovely house. Now, all anyone needs to know is I am your niece, Miss Grace Wilson. I live in London and will come visit now and again. No one needs to know more."

She nodded with a wink. "Oh, very well then, Poppy."

"I'll see to it that we have wood for a good fire tonight. I noticed a fine little store in the village but a mile up the path. I glanced around at the sparsely furnished little place with dingy white-washed walls. "I won't be long. I will make sure we have all the comforts of a snug, warm cottage. Pots, pans, utensils, blankets, chairs, pewterware ..."

Later that evening as I sat in front of the well-built fire, I watched Mary Agnes putter about the room. "Come now, do rest. Tomorrow will soon come."

✳ ✳ ✳

I awoke the following morning, Hawkeye lay curled in the corner. I could hear Mary Agnes snore and arose to make a nice pot of tea and warm the room. Trying to be very quiet I woke my dear little friend. "Come into the kitchen, I have made a fine breakfast, Mary Agnes."

We sat huddled near the fire drinking our tea. "It is a good day to plough, Poppy."

I nodded. "A very good day, Mary Agnes. And what will you plant, flowers or food?"

"Both."

"Ah, well then it is time for both."

"Now, in the morrow, you must go to that Peabury place and sort out your life, Poppy."

"I will, Mary Agnes." I pointed to the jar on the mantle ledge. "There is some money. Use what you need, dear friend."

I glanced out at the little patch of garden area, its rich black soil ready for sowing. "Indeed, the soil is ready for your hoe." I glanced up at the sky. "La, it looks like a rain shower is coming."

She smiled. "That's a good sign."

* * *

The next morning I waved goodbye to Mary Agnes and took the narrow path back to the village of Croydon, our new home. The walk to the train station was but a few miles west. I enjoyed the saunter as the weather remained mild, oh a few drops of rain now and again, but mild. A few passers-by nodded as I stood on the station waiting area. The clack from the train made me a little nervous betimes. The horses shied so; the cows hated the noise and smoke billowing wild and puffy as well. I worried so for the dogs running aside, barking. I imagined it hurt their ears as it did mine. Indeed, I rather preferred the coach.

Hawkeye remained standing, eyeing anyone who came too close. We boarded without incident this time. It was a short day's ride by train and then coach to reach Crawley, and then from there but a mile or so to Peabury. I climbed down, paid my fare, took what few belongings I had packed and walked back down into the village where I had begun my journey just a month prior.

I passed the house where Mrs Milbrew lived and paused. She did not come out into her garden, so I continued on. Reaching the top of the hill, I spied Peabury. A magnificent Great House. Would her ladyship accept me? I had kept an exact account of what I had spent thus far. Somehow and someway I will repay her generosity.

As I traversed the dusty blond pathway, I thought back to Mary Agnes. My heart was full and contented. The dear soul will have a place to live for the rest of her life in comfort. I laughed when I remembered when we first met in prison. The promise she made to return to the gin house where the owner broke her nose and had her taken off to jail—she was going to spit in his soup ... ha ha ha. I was giggling at such a thought when suddenly I heard the clatter of a wagon coming up from behind. La, it was Bessy at the reins, she was alone. I waved, and a great smile erupted on her tired face as she reined in Sugar.

"Grace, it be you?"

"Oh, yes, Bessy it is me all right." I petted Sugar on the nose. "I've missed you all a great deal." Hawkeye sniffed about the mare's hooves. "Careful, ol' boy. Mind that she remembers you."

"Climb up, climb up," cried Bessy, "the sun's a hot one today."

I hoisted Hawkeye up and climbed aboard. I hugged her in delight. "Where is your bonnet, Bessy? You'll mark your face."

"Oh, it blew off back aways, the devil about such nonsense. They be *my* freckles, right proud of 'em. Shows me not one of 'em white-faced ladies, that for sure."

I nodded. "Indeed. How have you been?"

"Same," she click-whistled, "move on, Sugar."

"Bessy, I have missed Peabury, you, Raven, Sugar ..."

"I noticed Hawkeye be seein' good with 'is one eye."

"Yes, it has grown together quite nicely, I must say. He somehow followed me when I left, Bessy. I didn't have time to take him back."

"Ah, he wouldn't of stayed all the same. He loves you, Poppy." She laughed. "I see'd that, so I did. You been takin' good care of him." She winked. "He'll never forget. Mind, he will look after ye forever."

"I suppose so."

"Where'd you been off to, Grace?"

"London, to find my mother."

She nodded. "I never had one, exceptin' to be borned by somebody."

"Well, I had a mother, but no father. I suppose we're the same."

She cackled, wiped the drool from her mouth, and glanced over at me. "No, Grace, we not the same."

"Bessy, you are very good. It matters little how fancy our words. It's our deeds that show our worth. I know it was you who saved me from Mrs Miles by fetching Lady Sheffield that day I was accused of stealing her ring. I never got a chance to thank you properly."

"Oh, I knowed you thankful."

I hugged her. "Very thankful."

The wagon was not as soft riding as my hired coach, but just being able to sit next to Bessy was worth the roughness. I retied my bonnet and took out my handkerchief and kept it to my face. "My, it's dusty today, Bessy."

"Ah, it be dusty every day exceptin' when it rains." She glanced up at the gathering grey clouds. "Maybe not so dusty soon." She laughed gesturing toward the sky.

She was right, and neither of us had an umbrella. She pulled under a great oak for shelter and let Sugar graze.

"What bring you back, Grace?"

"Well, I owe her ladyship a great debt of ... gratitude."

She nodded squinting out from under the drooping leaves while drops of rain plopped upon us now and again. The sound of thunder rolled far in the distance. The smell of freshly mowed hay wafted about the air.

"Before I return to London, I want to repay her."

"You goin' back as quick as you left, then?"

I laughed. "Yes, I have much yet to do there."

She shook her head. "I never wanna go there, Gracie."

"Well, have you ever been there?" I paused, glancing out from under the tree. "Oh, it is filled with noisy people hurrying here and there. And one must not dress in too much finery, or someone is apt to pick your pocket. The smell is quite disgusting—rudeness being the order of the day. I don't remember it ever being that way when I was a child. Even the flowers have lost their brilliance, but my life began there, Bessy. Part of my heart remains there somewhere, and I must find it."

"Well if part o' your heart is you mama's then maybe, but I never go'd there, Grace. Her ladyship wanted to take me to have my hip-bone attended there."

"What's wrong with your hip-bone, Bessy?"

"Oh, I be borned that way. Suppose I die that way, too."

"Dear me is that why you limp? Are you in pain?"

She shrugged. "Have to work." She glanced at me. "Jus' like you be working."

I nodded. "But I'm not in any pain, Bessy. Why didn't you allow her ladyship to take you to London?"

"Oh, no not there." Glancing out from under the tree, she noticed the rain had stopped and slapped the reins on Sugar's rump. "Once a cripple they no good. Just like his lordship when he go strange in the head they take him away."

I gasped. "They took Lord Sheffield away?"

"Oh, no, not him. They take *Lord Allenton* away."

"Lord Allenton? The physician, Dr Moore's father? He was at Peabury?"

She nodded. "I tole' you I knowed secrets, Grace."

"Where did they take him?"

"I heard them take him back to London. They takes everybody there ... to die. Jus' like you say, it not a nice place."

I sat there feeling terrible. A chill ran up my spine. Indeed, they took him back to his London townhouse, perhaps where I found him tied and gagged. What was I to do now? Return to London and bring Inspector Palgrave to Peabury? Oh, dear me, poor Bessy. "Have you told anyone else about what happened to his lordship, Bessy?"

She shook her head. "They dunno I knowed. My hip may be sore, but my eyes and ears work good." She glanced at me. "You be the only one I trust, Grace. I tole' nobody."

I nodded. "That's good, Bessy." I took her rough, calloused and red swollen hands into mine. They were little hands, shiny and cracked. As I thought of the kind physician, Dr Moore, my heart ached. I thought I was such a good judge of people. "Was his lordship's son in the scheme to take him away?"

She nodded.

My heart sank to the pit of my stomach. She must have read the expression on my face, for she quickly added:

"The older brother, Master George. Twasn't enough money to suit his fancy ways, methinks." She glanced out at the rutted road. "We better get on, Grace."

"What do you know of Mr Buffle, Bessy? Do you think he had anything to do with the disappearance of Lord Allenton?"

She click-whistled at Sugar to hurry along. "I think it to be, Grace." With squinty eyes, she wiped her mouth of spittle and went on, "He the butler, he knowed all things at Peabury."

And all things in London, as well, it seems.

My heart raced. "Did her ladyship know about his lordship leaving, Bessy?"

She shook her head. No, *our* ladyship dint know, but Lady Allenton did. I knowed that for true. I were workin' at her Great House in Bedfordshire helpin' in the kitchen."

"Bedfordshire, is that where his lordship's summer estate is?"

"Ah," she scratched her head, "methinks it were called Moorgate Manor."

"Moorgate Manor."

She nodded. " 'bout two hours by wagon." She pointed north. "Be that way."

"Is that where Dr Moore, the physician lives?"

"Moorgate? No. He dunno live there no more, but he was borned there. He goes a visiting some days. I heard him speak of it with her ladyship about growin' up as a boy."

I nodded. "No doubt rekindling fond memories." The wagon

continued to amble up the long hill. I only had a few moments left before we were in sight of the Great House. Should I jump off the wagon now and return to London and the inspector? Would Bessy be in harm? "Bessy, are you sure no one suspects you of knowing?"

She nodded. "They think me stupid, Grace."

Well, no harm has come to her thus far, but one never knows. "Bessy, you must come to me if you see or hear anything more."

She nodded.

"Bessy, I have a wee cottage in Croydon, it's a few hours from here, just outside London. It is a place where you could stay, forever—a safe, comfortable place. My good friend Mary Agnes Bennett lives there. She and I were in prison together."

Bessy's eyes grew wide.

"No worries, Bessy, I would trust her with my life. I have trusted her with my very life."

"Why you not stay with her now, Grace?"

"Someday, Bessy, but first I must pay my respects to her ladyship and then return to London, very soon."

She shook her head. "You be goin' back then to find you ma?"

"Yes, and there is much I cannot explain to you now, Bessy. However, I must return to London. Even though it seems I have never existed there. It is as if I was trying to match two pieces of cloth, but the stripes are off."

"Oh, now I knowed. Well, a day with Raven and Sugar will put the stripes together."

I felt her simple thinking settle goodness into my heart. "Indeed."

Just then Hawkeye barked. Jumping from the wagon, he raced out into the meadow. "He knows he's home, Bessy."

The wagon moved slowly around to the back of the barn at Peabury. Raven was sunning herself in the paddock, her black coat shined like satin. Sugar nickered, tossed her head, and swished her well-combed tail.

"I will find Mr Buffle and request to see her ladyship, Bessy." As I climbed down from the wagon, I stopped. "Bessy, does the name Mr Cooke sound familiar to you?"

She tied the reins to the brake-pull and stepped down. "That's another secret, Grace."

Chapter 9 – Peabury

As the stable boy came to unharness Sugar, Bessy took her brown, string-tied package from the wagon. Her voice dropped to a whisper, "Be talkin' to ye later, Grace."

"Later?"

"Well, well, what a pleasant surprise to find you here, Miss Wilson."

I turned at the familiar voice. "Oh, Dr Moore," I felt my face turn warm, "yes, I have come back … for a short visit to see her ladyship."

He handed the reins of his horse to one of the stable boys. "Come then, with me, I have an appointment with her within the hour." He smiled as he glanced over my new attire.

"I look like a real lady, I suppose, sir. I'm a wonder you recognised me."

"Well, besides your red hair, I …"

"Oh, well, then yes of course." I brushed away a dangling curl from my brow, and noticed Bessy hurrying into the servants' quarters.

"Will you be staying long, Miss Wilson? I waited for you at breakfast that morning after the wedding party. Imagine my surprise to learn you left in the middle of the night."

"I meant to leave you a note, sir. Forgive my hasty departure. It must have seemed rather odd of me, but it was a full moon, the sky cloudless, a rare opportunity to make my way to London."

He nodded politely. I sensed he wanted more of an explanation.

"I was becoming too accustomed to Peabury, sir. Had I not left when I did, perhaps I would have never gone."

"Indeed, to clear your reputation and find your mother, is that so, Miss Wilson?"

"Oh, yes, indeed, sir. That is precisely the reason."

"And did you get to the bottom of it?"

I knew he was curious, but I had promised Inspector Palgrave not to say a word. "To the bottom of it? Well, no, sir, but

I will return to London very soon. There are some things I must continue to research—but, no, sir, I have not found my mother."

"You have come back for …?"

"To pay her ladyship a visit, Dr Moore, and then I shall be on my way once more."

"Walking?"

I nodded. "Only until I reach the village sir, the London stagecoach stops there."

"I see." He seemed to ponder my words then he glanced up at the entryway into the Great House. "Well, here we are then."

He gestured for me to enter.

"I wonder if I should find Mr Buffle and present myself properly, Dr Moore. Perhaps her ladyship would not take to me barging in, so to speak."

"She has missed you, you know, Miss Wilson. I do not think she would object in the least. And besides, I think it best if we sidestep Mr Buffle for the time being."

What could he mean? I nodded, looking directly into his eyes. "Very well, sir."

We traversed the long shiny wooden hallway floors and soon came to what Dr Moore said was the music room. With a slight tap at the door, we heard her ladyship beckon us to enter.

"Why, Grace," said her ladyship as she anxiously rose from the piano stool and took my hands, "how very nice to see you. When did you come? Just now? Why, I did not hear a carriage approach. Oh, but I've been playing …"

"I rode in the wagon with Bessy, your ladyship. I met up with her on the village road."

"Bessy? Was she out this morning?" She glanced up at the chandelier and nodded. "Yes, I suppose so." She pulled the bell-pull and took my hand. "Come sit, tell me about your travels. We'll have a nice cup of tea."

Dr Moore hemmed. "Excuse me, Aunt Catherine, but I have come to see you as well. You must remember our weekly appointment?" He seemed to be teasing her. "Although I am, no doubt, not as charming as Miss Wilson, but I really must examine your spine before I am dismissed for lack of intrigues and the latest London gossip from our friend."

"Well, Patty, as you can see, I am very well. I can, at least now, sit comfortably at the piano for an entire hour without tiring."

"Then I am dismissed, is it?"

"Take a chair, Patrick and do be mindful of my little animal girl. You shall have tea with us."

Dr Moore did not hesitate to sit, and very near me, I might add. I could feel my face warm again and withdrew my fan. *Why do I warm so around him?*

"Oh, what a lovely lace fan, my dear. Let me see it," said her ladyship as I handed it to her. She studied it closely. "Very nice, indeed. I can always judge a well-bred lady by her fans. You have exquisite taste, my dear. Which London shop did you buy it?"

I thought for a moment. "I do not remember your ladyship, but you may keep it, ma'am. I would be honoured if you did."

She smiled. "Oh, I would not think of such a thing, my dear. How very kind you are."

Dr Moore hemmed. "How is Hawkeye, Miss Wilson? You know after you left the ol' cur disappeared and we assumed ..."

"He found me, Dr Moore, miles along the London Road. How miraculous it was to me, but I could not retrace my steps to bring him back." I glanced up at her ladyship. "You must understand. I did not take him."

"Oh, indeed." Dr Moore nodded apologetically. "I did not mean to imply ..."

Her ladyship smiled. "I do not follow the whereabouts of the hounds, Grace, I assure you. I suppose he simply ran after you. After all, you did save his life. He is yours, my dear."

"Thank you, your ladyship." I glanced over at Dr Moore. "But, sir, you were the one who saved his life, not me."

"Well, now, I must say, if you had not kept him calm that day under the bush, he would have ripped me to shreds. Indeed, the ol' cur adores you, Miss Wilson."

Her ladyship turned her attention to her nephew. "Well, Patrick, who could not adore Miss Wilson?"

His face reddened. Smiling, he nodded. "Indeed."

I did not fully comprehend the hidden meaning of her ladyship's remark that morning until a few months later. And then I learned just how *adoring* Dr Moore had become.

"While on the road, sir, I took great care to keep his head bandaged. An apothecary examined him as well. Hawkeye is now free of all bandages, and his eye is completely healed. He travels very well by the way, and quite the protector, I must say."

Her ladyship smiled. "Well, indeed."

A servant arrived with the tea tray, making tiny noises as she readied everything. Fine white napkins aside a lovely pink rosebud in an exquisite little crystal vase sat in the middle of the silver tray.

I made polite conversation, but all the while I contemplated how I was to thank her ladyship for slipping such a sum into my purse.

"Aunt, if it pleases you, it would only take me a moment to examine your spine." He took a few pillows and put them at her back. "You must remember to keep it straight at all times."

"Oh, indeed, Patty, but it is feeling so much the better ..."

"Well, it is important that you follow my instructions and it will remain that way."

She raised her brows. "Well, I have been reprimanded it seems, Miss Wilson." Squirming in her chair, she comforted herself with a pillow. "However shall I get along without him?"

I nodded. "Ma'am, it would serve you well if you listened to his advice."

Both she and doctor exchanged glances and then stared at me.

"Oh, forgive me, your ladyship. It is that I am very fond of you and could not bear it if you became crippled by your injuries."

"Crippled? Dear me, I think not," she countered. "It is only a minor ..."

"Not so fast, Aunt Catherine. Spine injuries can cause catastrophic malformations. Miss Wilson is right. I, too, could not bear it to see you ... hunched over ... with a cane, perhaps."

I believe at this point, he was trying to scare her ladyship into listening to his advice. I glanced over at her. Her mouth gaped. She set down her teacup with a clatter.

"Hunched over? A limp?" she glanced at him with a wry smile. "Very well, you two, I shall remember my pillows whenever I travel."

"That's the spirit, dearest Aunt." He kissed her cheek. "Now, you must dismiss me for I have things I must attend to. I'll be back within the hour for your exercises." He smiled at me. "Anyway, I sense Miss Wilson would like a little time with you, alone."

Her ladyship nodded. "Very well, Patty." She glanced at the mantle clock. "His lordship will be expecting me for high tea. Do be on time, dear."

Dr Moore smiled at me. "I do hope to see you again, soon, Miss Wilson. Are you staying at Peabury for a while?"

I glanced at her ladyship, unsure just what she would do with me. "Ah, sir, I am not exactly sure how long I shall stay."

He half-bowed. "Well then, I will have Aunt keep me informed of your visit."

"Indeed, sir."

Before he closed the door behind him, he paused. "I think I will find Mr Hawkeye and take a good look at his eye."

"Oh, thank you, sir. I should like that very much."

Her ladyship tapped my hand. "Tell me, Grace, just what are your plans?"

I lowered my voice. "Your ladyship, I returned to thank you for the huge sum of money you slipped into my purse the night I left Peabury. It was a ..."

"Money?" She drew back, "why, Grace, I did no such thing."

Chapter 10 – Bessy Shares a Secret

Her ladyship insisted I stay at Peabury for the week, but I was anxious to return to London and expressed my concern to her, and particularly my disbelief at the huge sum of money deposited into my purse by whom, I was not at all sure, dumbfounded, however, all the same.

"Grace," she poo-pooed, "someone felt you deserved such a sum. You must be gracious and just be happy over it."

"Oh, your ladyship I could not do such a thing."

She tweaked my cheek. "Very well then, think as you wish, but I'll not hear another word of it. Promise me, Grace."

I dropped my head. I knew I had become a great bore. "Very well, your ladyship, I shall never mention the money again."

"Very well, then." She glanced at my pouty face and tweaked my nose. "Grace, if I do come to learn of the donor, I shall tell you."

"Oh, your ladyship I would be most grateful if you did."

"Well, then, let us be done with it. So, what say you we take a ride tomorrow and have a picnic. Raven will remember you and be on her best behaviour."

"Oh, that would be splendid, ma'am. I would love that."

Later that evening, on my way to my room, I thought about Bessy and decided to pay her a visit in the servants' quarters. It was just past ten, and I knew she was the last servant to leave the kitchen. I was anxious to learn what she knew of Mr Cooke. Just how many more secrets had she stored under that little day cap of hers, I was wondering.

Quietly descending the back stairs, I was cautious not to bump into Mr Buffle. I found her scrubbing the floor. Poor soul, I should love to take her with me to Mary Agnes and there she would have an easy life and a good friend. "Bessy," I whispered glancing around, "are you near finished?"

She threw the scrub brush into her bucket and stood holding her back. "What you be doin' here, Gracie? You hungry?"

"Oh, no, I just need to speak with you ... regarding Mr

Cooke."

She nodded. "I'll finish here and meet you under the great yew, just near the carriage-porch."

I nodded and left.

Bessy found me just about the same time as Hawkeye. The evening sky was a deep lavender, the trees dark against the purple landscape. It was a mild evening with a slight breeze. We sat on the white settee in the garden.

"You must be exhausted my dear girl," I said to Bessy as she tucked a loose lock of hair up under her cap.

"Oh, me used to it, Gracie." She wiped her mouth with the back of her hand. "What I knowed about Mr Cooke is he be the butler at Moorgate. Always been kind to us. He left one day after his lordship Allenton wandered off somewhere and didn't come back for hours. He were mighty worried, more than anybody. Then he was disgusted at the lot of them for not caring for his lordship with a proper physician. One day a lady came to Moorgate, and Cooke left with her. That's the last we seed him."

"Mr Cooke was upset that no one took good care of Lord Allenton, is that it, Bessy?"

She nodded. "Cooke thought mighty high of his lordship and took good care of the old one, but her ladyship always been interferin' with him. So he left disgusted."

"What about Dr Moore? He was a physician. Surely he would have taken good care of his own father?"

"Oh, he weren't no doctor then, Grace. He helped his father where he could, but when he left for school, they be ignoring his lordship again."

"You say a lady showed up one day and Mr Cooke left with her?"

She nodded. "That he did, Gracie."

I was confounded by the developments. "Did he say where he was going?"

"Me figure London. There's where his mother live, but I could be wrong, mind you. She dead by now, thinking to meself, she be old."

I nodded. "And you haven't heard anything since?"

"No, but nobody says nothin' to me. I just listen."

I hugged her. "Thank you, good Bessy. I took her hand. "Bessy, have you given any thought to returning to Croydon with me? You could stay there for the rest of your life. I worry about you here."

Her mouth dropped. "Oh, holy fish, Gracie, I dunno of such

a thing. Scrubbin' floors is all I knowed."

"Well, you'd probably have to scrub a few with Mary Agnes, hoe the garden, milk the cow, but I'm sure you'd have a wonderful life there. I plan on returning once I find Mama. Think of it, we could be family, Bessy."

Tears sprung from her tired eyes. "Family?"

I nodded. "You must return with me, ol' girl. In a few years, you'll be spent and then what?"

She took my hand. "I canno leave this week, Gracie, come back for me next month?"

I hugged her. "That I will."

* * *

I left Peabury for London that following week. Her ladyship insisted upon my taking her carriage at least to the village. Oh, I felt quite grand sitting high and mighty in her carriage. I watched the meadows and hay fields stretch out before me. The sun's rays were squinty bright. A few cows meandered in a distant field, they were South Devons, if I remember correctly. I took in a great breath and felt happy inside. The sky a brilliant white, a few clouds streamed into long rows of misty vapour. Indeed it was a beautiful day.

I felt anxious to see Mary Agnes. I do not know why I worry about her so. She can certainly well manage any sort of circumstance. Won't she be surprised to learn of Bessy joining our little family? Clutching my purse, I felt the bundle of money neatly tied with a blue satin ribbon. Well, I certainly have enough to add another room. Smiling, I glanced down at Hawk. "So, my good man, did you find your visit to Peabury to your liking?"

He glanced up at me with a wiggle.

"Good. I am happy for you," I tied the drawstrings to my wrist. "Now, if I could only find who put that sum of money in my purse, I will certainly be happy over it. Sometimes fortunes find their way in the strangest fashion, and this is a very strange one, indeed. I petted his head. "I am happy you chose to travel with me again, ol' boy. One never knows who's going to board the coach anymore. And I still have a great deal of money. Oh, how am I to repay such a sum? And, more importantly, to whom?"

When we reached the village, I had just reached for the doorknob when the footman opened the door.

"Beg pardon, madam. I was instructed to wait until you were

safe aboard the Londoner." He glanced at his watch. "It should be here within quarter of the hour, Miss Wilson."

"Oh." I sat back. "Well, then, Hawk we'll just wait, I suppose." I glanced at the attentive footman. "How very kind of her ladyship to be so thoughtful."

I was staring out the window at nothing in particular when I heard a tap tap at the opposite window. There was Dr Moore looking in, shielding his eyes from the noonday sun, his whip dangling from his wrist.

"I say, Miss Wilson, you've gone off again without saying goodbye." A silly grin spread across his face.

Hawkeye wiggled his entire wiry little body.

"Oh, sir, do come in. I've a few minutes before the Londoner arrives."

He tipped his hat and smiled. "Don't mind if I do, miss."

Climbing into the cab, he sat across from me. Settling in his seat, he removed his hat and set it next to him. "Well, now, thank you for inviting me in. Now we don't have to shout."

I giggled. "Oh, I am certain the villagers enjoyed the banter, sir."

He nodded. "Indeed, they live from week to week for a tidbit or two—particularly from the Peabury visitors."

"Yes, I would imagine."

"Oh, indeed so." Reaching over, he rubbed Hawk's ears. "Ah, old boy, followed her again did you?"

"I do not know how he does such a thing, sir. The minute the coach came round the carriage-porch to fetch me he was at my side." I smiled. "And I am very grateful, he is a wonderful companion."

"Indeed, it is good to have such a friend when you're travelling alone. You must be ever vigilant, Miss Wilson." His face turned serious.

I was a little taken aback by his concern. "Why, indeed, sir, but not to worry, I can take care of myself."

He scoffed. "Oh, I hear that from many of my patients." He twirled his hat examining its brim in detail. With a frown, he looked into my eyes. "And the highways are rife with scoundrels anymore. With a pocket full of money, I would be very careful in not exhibiting a penny more than necessary."

I must have had an odd look when he put his hat back on. "Her ladyship informed me of your inheritance, Miss Wilson. I did not mean to pry, I assure you."

"My inheritance, sir?" I frowned. "I would not call it that, for

I do not know who slipped it into my purse and I am in constant wonder at who would do such a thing."

"Londoner, Miss Wilson, approaching. Londoner," said the footman.

Dr Moore stepped out and took my hand to help me down. "Do be careful, Miss Wilson. I would have been more than happy to escort you into London, but my patients, you see, are waiting."

I was more than touched at his sincerity. I could feel my face warm. Certainly I was not used to such gentlemanly conduct and didn't know exactly what to say. "Well, sir, of course your patients await your most excellent care. I would never have expected that you leave them behind—least not on my account. But thank you for your kind thoughts."

"When will you return, Miss Wilson?"

Just then a loud whistle and shouts came from an impatient groom who sat atop his box on the Londoner coachwhip in hand. "Hurry along! Hurry along!"

"Is he shouting at me?"

Peabury's groom raised his fist. "Hold your tongue. Her ladyship will be there when she's ready and not a minute less," he growled.

Everybody in the stagecoach stared out the window. Those atop gawked.

"Oh, dear me, Dr Moore, I have caused a scene."

"No worries, Miss Wilson. Let them think you're a grand dame. They'll be more than anxious to make way for you, and not give you grief about Hawkeye in the bargain."

I hurried to the stagecoach, and just as I was about to step up, I smiled and waved to Dr Moore. "Good-bye, sir."

He touched the brim of his hat with a nod and smiled. "Perhaps then, London, Lady Grace."

Oh, dear me, now I'm Lady Grace? One silly falsehood after the other, that's my score. Pretty soon I'll begin to believe such a lie. Taking my seat, I noticed those that had been sitting on my side were all bunched together on the other. They had made way for a fine lady, perhaps from some great house nearby. They wanted to ask me why I didn't take the fancy barouche I had just left, but knew better than ask. Hawkeye pushed in at my skirt, he wanted his leash to be removed.

"No, my dear boy, you must stay at my command and wishes at all times. I will not untie you."

Everyone's eyes settled upon Hawkeye's sealed, wrinkly eye socket, and then in unison they glanced back up into mine. I leaned down and kissed Hawkeye's bumpy little head. "My darling little man, how I adore you."

It was near 6 o'clock that evening when I picked up my small portmanteau and sauntered up the narrow lane toward the cottage but a mile distant from the busy village of Croydon. From a small clearing, I spied our little place and unleashed Hawkeye. "Run now, dear boy." I watched after him as he knew exactly where our little place was situated.

Mary Agnes stood at the open doorway. An apron tied about her ample bosom, a warm smile made way on her tanned, wrinkled face. Her hair was wrapped up and stuck with a tortoiseshell comb. I sniffed the air. "Well, I have arrived in perfect time."

She hugged me. "Poppy girl, yes, perfect time. I was 'bout to seed the garden, but will do it in the morrow." She looked me up and down. "Well, I see you are still clutching that fat purse of yours."

I carefully lay it onto a kitchen chair. "Oh, well, yes. That's all we have in the world, Mary Agnes." I glanced around the little cottage. "Well, you've made a sweet home here, indeed, all neat and tidy. Where did you find the table and chairs?" I ran my hand over its smooth surface. "La, but it is well made and shiny."

I hoed a garden for an ol' spinster up the lane, swept some cobwebs from her windows, and made her a pot o' stew."

"Well done." I glanced at the stew pot hanging over the fire and sniffed the air. "And you kept some for yourself?"

"No, I be expectin' ya to be returnin' soon and made another pot." She stirred it with a long twisted spoon, sniffing the air. "It be done, Poppy if you be hungry."

"Hungry?" I glanced over at the bubbling stew. "I am famished."

I grabbed a bowl and held it for her to fill. "To the brim—ah, yes, there's a girl."

We both sat and watched Hawkeye lay down by the hearth, but first, he begged for a morsel or two. I tossed him a pinch of bread. "You'll be fed later, ol' boy."

"Did he keep the wolves away again, Poppy?"

"Well, I suppose he did." I spooned into my broth. "Mary Agnes, you know all along I thought her ladyship put that money into my purse ..."

"She din't?"

I shook my head. "And I am at a loss as to who put it there." I set down my spoon. "Do you think someone put it there by mistake?"

"No, somebody love you, Poppy."

"Love me? Indeed not. No one there even knows me. It's certainly not Mr Snivel, and I know beyond a doubt it was not the housekeeper. Let us rule out his lordship. He thinks I'd make a fine stable boy. And then there is Dr Moore, the physician."

Mary Agnes looked up at me. "What about 'im, dearie?"

"No, he just sent his mother his life's savings ..."

"Well, Poppy maybe whoever put it there don't care if ye pay it back, sounds like that to me."

"Yes, that is what her ladyship said as well, and I am beginning to think that way, Mary Agnes. She said if she found the donor she would tell me. All the same, I will spend a month more in London, and if I have not found what I am looking for, I shall return."

Mary Agnes smiled, her crooked teeth yellow, edged brown, but strong; her crinkly brown eyes set deep beneath her furrowed brow. "That sounds the best of plans, Poppy."

"Oh, dear me Mary Agnes, I must tell you we may have another friend join us here in our little cottage."

"To live?"

"Mary Agnes, she's the scullery maid at Peabury—you'll love her as I do. Her name is Bessy."

"Oh, you be picking up strays again, so you have," she laughed.

"Oh, indeed."

I explained what a great help Bessy was and all the secrets she shared with me, and her bad hip-bone.

"Perhaps within the month, we'll be family, Mary Agnes. I will be leaving for London in the morning." I explained about Mr Cooke and what little I gleaned from Bessy regarding him. "But, Mary Agnes, I have the strangest feeling she's withheld something more about him, and I aim to find out more."

Chapter 11 – Poppy Returns to Inspector Palgrave

Hawk and I arrived in London on Thursday, 6 July, my birthday. Turning twenty-three only made me feel more of a spinster. I had hoped for a good husband and many children by then, but reckoned that would have to wait, even, perhaps, for an eternity.

"This way, Hawkeye." I led him from the coach and out onto Fenchurch Street where I hailed a gig and was delivered to the Mivart again. It was a very nice hotel, and I found the accommodations very much to our liking. I was in need of a few more frocks and bonnets to continue my search, however. I learned that one must dress properly to ask questions and expect immediate and proper answers.

Passing a dress shop on Grace Church Street, I spied a lovely lavender frock with a fancy feathered hat, and then a white muslin with red dots would do very nicely. I paid the sum and returned to my room. Pulling from the package a bone, I patted Hawk's head. "Here you are, my good man. You must enjoy it, for the butcher was to give it to *his* hound, but I talked him out of doing such a thing, quite persuasively, I must say."

I sent off a note to Inspector Palgrave informing him I had returned to London and that I had some news to share with him. I was in hopes he had made some progress in his search for my mother. My latest news regarding his lordship would be quite astounding, I was sure of it.

Thinking of what Bessy had told me regarding what she remembered, I worried that somehow her ladyship and his lordship would be dragged into a quagmire of debauchery, and for that, I was feeling very unsettled. And worried as well, that the good doctor, Dr Moore, would also be drawn into the intrigue, but I had no choice in the matter.

* * *

Inspector Palgrave met me in the lobby at ten o'clock the following morning. I was standing at the palm frond near the front desk when Hawk suddenly began whining and wiggling.

"Oh, sir, Inspector, I am so happy to see you, sir."

He knelt down to inspect Hawk's eye. "Healed very nicely, I see."

"Oh, yes indeed, and look how his tail wags. He's more than happy to see you, sir. And so am I."

"Had an eventful visit to Peabury, did you?"

"Oh, indeed, sir." I glanced around covering my mouth with my fan. "And I've gathered a considerable amount of intrigue."

"Intrigue, you say? Well, then, I must hear it." He returned his hat to his head. "Let us be off to the Yard."

Together we entered his austere office. "Oh, it is all quite proper here, sir."

"Proper?" He hung his hat and umbrella on the coatrack. Glancing around he said, "I suppose so."

We sat in unison.

"Well, now, Miss Wilson you must share with me your latest *intrigue*."

I relayed to him what Bessy had told me regarding Mr Cooke, and that he apparently cared for Lord Allenton, but a woman came to call one day, and he left with her, returning to London perhaps. I explained that Bessy had worked at Moorgate Manor and his lordship's second son, Dr Moore, loved his father apparently, however, when away at school his father was mistreated.

Feeling a surge of love for poor ol' Bessy, I blurted: "I shall have Bessy come live with us, Inspector."

He abruptly turned in his chair with such a look. "Live with *us*, Miss Wilson? Live where?"

"Oh, forgive my outburst, sir. I forgot to mention that when we last parted, on my way back to the Mivart Hotel, I miraculously found Mary Agnes Bennett."

"Your prison mate?"

"Indeed, sir. She was crossing the street when I spied her. I promptly jumped from the coach and hurried to her side."

He shook his head. "You've taken in another stray, I see."

"I opened my little drawstring purse and showed him the huge roll of money still left. "But sir, I have so much money, so I bought a wee cottage just outside London, Inspector, on the road to Peabury. I left Mary Agnes there and promised to return soon. Oh, sir, now poor Bessy has a bad hip-bone and ..."

"Now, now Miss Wilson, I do understand the predicament."

He smiled. "So, you are to bring this Bessy back to your little cottage? And in what village is this little cottage again?"

"Oh, I am not sure of its name, sir. Croydon or something ... Oh, yes, that's it, Croydon."

"Croydon, yes, nice that you could remember its name, Miss Wilson. Easier to find your way back."

"Oh, indeed, sir."

"Yes, and I hope you still have a few pennies to your name. I take it you did not stay at Peabury to work off what you have spent thus far?"

"Oh, the money is another matter entirely, sir. I forgot to mention that as well."

"Forgot to mention, what, Miss Wilson?"

"The money, sir. Lady Sheffield denied putting such a sum into my little purse."

The inspector slowly closed his eyes, shaking his head.

"I know this all sounds so terribly bizarre, sir." I sighed heavily and scooted back into my chair. "What am I to make of it all?"

"Let me examine that roll of paper you have wadded up there in your little drawstring purse, Miss Wilson. That is, what is left."

"Oh, indeed, but I've hardly made the slightest dent in it, sir."

I watched as he carefully flattened and straightened the paper as he counted each note, placing the currency in neat little piles. He would occasionally sigh as he glanced up into my questioning face. "This is a very considerable sum, Miss Wilson. Have you counted it?"

"Oh, no, sir. I only removed what I needed ... when I needed it. But I have no idea exactly how much is there."

"Five thousand pounds and a few coins, *not* being exact, Miss Wilson."

"Oh ... five thousand pounds, indeed, five thousand pounds, inspector—why that is a huge sum of money—oh, dear me."

"Indeed, dear me."

"Her ladyship said if she perhaps came to overhear who put that sum into my purse she would tell me. Isn't that good news, sir?"

"I hardly think she will 'overhear' any such conversation, Miss Wilson."

My spirits dashed suddenly. I could feel my cheeks redden. "Oh."

"No good in pouting, Miss Wilson. Whoever gave you that money will no doubt remain anonymous. I suggest putting the majority of it in the bank, for safe keeping."

I nodded. "Well, yes, that does sound like a very good idea, sir."

"We shall do that right now." He stood. "This way, Miss Wilson."

* * *

After the deposit, I was left with one hundred pounds. "I feel much safer now, Inspector."

"You *are* safer now, Miss Wilson."

"Why, I don't know why I didn't think of such a thing first off." I frowned.

"Tell me about this Bessy, Miss Wilson."

"Well, sir, I learned that she knew Mr Cooke."

"Mr Cooke, the ring you found in your pocket in London, Mr Cooke?"

"Yes, sir, and apparently he was a very good butler to Lord Allenton. Bessy helped in the kitchen for a little while at Mooregate Manor ..."

"Mooregate Manor, indeed, and I believe that was Lord Allenton's summer estate. Let me see, she was a scullery maid at Peabury and occasionally helped in service at Moorgate. Is that correct, Miss Wilson?"

Why, the inspector has a most excellent sense of categorising people he does not even know. "Yes, sir, she helped at Moorgate now and again when there was a ball. Good help is very hard to find, sir. She helped in the kitchen, and that's how she got to know Mr Cooke."

"Do you know of this lady who came to visit Mr Cooke?"

I shook my head. "Ah, the one that he left with, sir?"

"The very one."

"No, sir, Bessy just mentioned it in passing."

"I see."

"Sir, you must return to Peabury with me. You grasp very well the intentions of those whom I have mentioned. Her ladyship would find you ... entertaining."

"Entertaining you say?" He scoffed. "So, a Scotland Yard Detective is labelled entertaining."

"Oh, I did not mean entertaining in a whimsical may or a demeaning way, sir. I meant full of insights, no rubbish in the pea-pot ..."

"Pea-pot?"

I pointed to my head with a laugh. "Mama used to rap my head with her knuckles when I'd prattle on so. She called it my pea-pot."

"Hmm."

His mouth resisted a smile. "Pea-pot, indeed. I shall remember that, Miss Wilson."

"Oh, I know you will, sir."

"Well then, perhaps I *will* pay Lady Allenton a visit."

"Lady Sheffield, sir."

"Yes, that's right, Lady Sheffield."

"When would you like to go?"

"Tomorrow would do very nicely."

"Oh, very good, sir. On the way, we shall stop and visit with Mary Agnes. You will see our little cottage, our cow and the chickens. You will see ..."

He hemmed. "Yes, yes, Miss Wilson, we shall stop for a visit. The name Poppy came to you as a flower girl, if I remember correctly? And Lord Sheffield used to buy your poppies."

"Lord Allenton, sir, used to buy my daisies."

"Oh, yes. How confusing I can make things betimes."

I looked at him studying his crinkly blue eyes and knew very well he would not do such a thing. Inspector Palgrave was much too smart to confuse anyone with anything out of order.

"So, you do not believe that I can become confused? I see by the look on your face, Miss Wilson, that you do not."

"No, sir, you know precisely who each individual I have presented to you is and where they live and what they do. You shall not convince me otherwise. You are much too brilliant to do anything less."

He shook his head. "Well, finally someone who sees directly through me. I have been found out at last. And to think it took a Poppy Pea-Pot to sort me out entirely."

I busted out into a fit of giggles, tears rolled from my eyes. Hawkeye came running jumping onto my lap. Licking my face, I laughed harder. Soon the inspector was guffawing as well.

One of his sergeants tapped on his office door and stepped in finding us both having a good laugh of it. He frowned and retreated, closing the door quietly behind him.

The inspector glanced around his austere office. "I don't laugh much, Miss Wilson. Not much in the way of whimsy visits me here."

"Sir," I dabbed my eyes, "I haven't laughed this loud since I was a wee child. Ah, I feel so happy inside."

"Yes, well, laughter will sometimes do that." He stood and glanced outside. "It looks like rain. I'll hail a coach for you and see you in the lobby at 6 a.m. sharp, tomorrow morning."

"Oh, indeed, inspector. Mary Agnes will be more than delighted to meet you. Perhaps a little apprehensive at meeting a policeman, but she'll warm."

* * *

Six a.m. sharp was exactly that, perhaps a little too sharp, but I managed to waken, brush my hair and get dressed. I reckoned the inspector was someone not to be left waiting. Descending the stairs into the lobby, I spied him waiting at the entryway.

"Good morning, sir."

"Good morning, Miss Wilson. I have a coach waiting."

While traversing the London Road toward Croydon, about a mile distant, I suddenly remembered that dastardly O'Malacy's odd remark about Mr Buffle as he was pulling Lord Allenton and me rudely up the ally. "Sir, I have suddenly remembered something quite astonishing." Hawkeye whined as he jumped up on the vacant seat next to me.

"Go on, Miss Wilson."

"Sir, do you remember when I, and his lordship, were arrested in the alley just behind Lord Allenton's Great House by the policeman O'Malacy?"

"Was it when he put the ring in his purse?"

"Yes, that's right Inspector. Mr O'Malacy was pulling me up the alley by my braid, pushing his lordship alongside. I was crying to be set free. I glanced back and spied Mr Buffle standing a great distance behind us. He stood watching all the while. I cried out to him to vouchsafe for us ..."

"Dear me, what did he do?"

"Nothing, sir, but just stared after us. When Mr O'Malacy caught sight of Mr Buffle watching after us, he scoffed."

"Scoffed?"

"Oh, Indeed, inspector, he said: 'That man is not Mr Buffle.' "

"Hmm, indeed." He withdrew from his inner vest pocket a little brown leather tablet, worn and tattered. First licking his thumb, he flipped through a few pages, read a few lines, glanced up into my face and nodded. "So noted, Miss Wilson."

"Is that not an important recollection, sir?"

"Extremely relevant, of course. Please continue to inform me of any further recollections, Miss Wilson."

"Oh, indeed, sir. I am thankful you are not ill-tempered toward me at such sudden recollections." Glancing out the window, I shook my head. "I wonder what else will bubble up."

"Well, you'll be at my side when I interrogate, I mean *speak* with her ladyship. Sometimes just a spoken word will evoke a memory."

"Will you *speak* with everyone at Peabury, sir?"

His chin lifted ever so slightly and with a slight nod, replied, "I plan on speaking with everyone, and in case you are not aware of my line of questions, Miss Wilson, I will not brow-beat anyone into any false confessions."

False confessions? Oh, dear me, I gulped. My eyes must have widened considerably. I stroked Hawkeye's little head burying my face into his fur. Glancing up I noticed a twinkle in the inspector's eye. "Oh, sir, you delight in teasing me."

"Well, as you, no doubt, have noticed I am subtle in my approach, but I have my ways of delving into this and that. I am quite adept at spotting false faces."

"Oh, indeed, sir, you wouldn't have come with me thus far had I been anything but forthright." I hugged Hawkeye. "Oh, sir, I cannot wait to find the missing pieces to my puzzling life—and the dear Lord Allenton. Oh, I pray he is still alive." Tears dripped freely down my face and atop Hawk's sweet little head. "Will I ever find Mama?"

He handed me his pocket handkerchief. "I am not one to promise anything, my dear. I've not been met with as many obstacles in my career as the ones you've presented to me thus far. However, I, like Hawkeye, will keep digging."

"Oh, indeed, sir."

Chapter 12 – Peabury and Scotland Yard

Approaching Croydon, I pointed in the direction of my little cottage. Unleashing Hawkeye, I stepped back. "He'll show us way, sir."

"Hmm," sighed Palgrave, "through the thickets no doubt."

Winding our way down a narrow pathway, we spied our little place nestled amongst a copse of oaks. In the distance were neat rows of hoed black soil deftly turned and mulched, surrounded by freshly planted flowers not yet in bloom. An old hedgerow grew wild at the back of our fieldstone house, no doubt blocking the north winds.

When we entered the cottage I found everything neat and tidy, but no Mary Agnes. "Well, sir, she must be in the village." I hung my cloak on a wall peg. "Allow me to take your coat, sir. Please, sit while I heat a kettle for tea."

"Oh, I'd rather snoop about ... if you don't mind, that is."

"Oh, indeed not, sir." I watched as he stooped under the low doorway and walked back outside, twirling his hat. I lost track of him while I fetched teacups, spoons and all the necessaries for a light lunch. Mary Agnes had all the utensils, pewterware, pots and pans neatly stacked on the sideboard. I thought her to be a very tidy person, I welcomed that indeed. I tended to be messy and altogether unsorted.

Opening the window in the kitchen, I stuck my head out and was met with Hawkeye jumping onto the ledge. "Well, ol' boy, I can see by your muddy paws you are enjoying your jaunt. Have you run into Mary Agnes by chance?"

"Oh, now, Poppy," Mary Agnes said bustling to my side, "that little cur was too busy trying to catch a fish to notice me."

Shooing him off the ledge, I closed the window. "Indeed, Mary Agnes, why I have brought along a ..."

"Oh, I already met him. He were inspecting me garden, pointing out where I'd forgot piling me some water stones." She took my arm whispering, "I smell *squire* on him, Poppy. Be about your wits, girl."

Giggling, I hugged her. "You are near right old girl. He's a detective from Scotland Yard. No fear, he knows all about us."

She glanced out the open door shaking her head. "I dunno trust any of 'em, Poppy."

"I know, Mary Agnes, but this one you can." I was met with a wry smile. "No, you must believe me, he is trustworthy. I bet my life on him, my dear old girl, actually *our* lives."

Detective Palgrave entered with a polite knock. "Good afternoon, ladies. He nodded to Mary Agnes. "You must be Mary Agnes. May I address you informally, madam?"

She curtsied with a blush. "Oh, indeed, sire. You call me Mary Agnes."

I put my arm around her waist. "No need to curtsey, Mary Agnes."

"Well, actually I rather like the formality," said Palgrave with a tiny smile. "Rather suits me, I would say."

Hawkeye whined.

"What is that you say, hound?" Palgrave teasingly shook his finger at him. "I'll have you know I am a detective of great significance." He shot a glance at me.

"Oh, yes, indeed, sir."

Mary Agnes fanned her face with her apron. "Donno manners, sire, but I knowed about fixing dinner."

"Oh, indeed, Miss Wilson has bragged about your culinary ..."

"No meaning interrupting sire, but I dunno *culiney*, just cooking."

"Well, yes, indeed then, cooking it is." Palgrave took a seat in front of the fire. "Make no fuss, madam. I am not a picky eater."

"Well, I knowed by yer skinny legs you be a picky about somethin' or other."

My jaw dropped. "Mary Agnes, really now. You mustn't insult our guest."

Palgrave laughed lightly. "No worries, Miss Wilson, she simply speaks from the heart. Her words flow honestly. Honestly in any form is agreeable to me. Go about your cooking now after which I will take a room in the village. We should get an early start for Peabury tomorrow, Miss Wilson."

✳ ✳ ✳

The next morning I met the inspector at the London Road,

and the path up into the village of Croydon was a muddy one. It had rained earlier, and though the air was heavy with moistness, it was cool and mild. Stopping to catch my breath, I fanned my warm face. "Inspector, we'll be able to take the coach to Crawley and then walk to Peabury from there."

Studying his muddy boots, he nodded. "We'll see."

Halfway up the path, I stopped to take in a great breath. "Poor Hawkeye, I feel sorry for him. He must feel abandoned."

"Perhaps not, Miss Wilson."

"What do you mean, sir?"

"He's been tailing us for the last mile."

I turned and caught sight of the little mite as he dashed into the woods. He knew I had spied him. "Come along, Hawk," I shouted and waved. "Come along, now."

With his tail between his legs, he wiggled up to us. "You naughty boy, poor Mary Agnes will think you ran off." I patted his matted head. "Well," I cooed, "I must say I'm happy you found us."

"Come along, you two. I would like to reach the train station before it darkens."

"Oh, indeed, sir. Once into Crawley, there is a fine place there, I noticed when riding through town. It is called The White Hart Inn. The stagecoach stops there many times a day."

"It is on the London Road then?"

"Oh, yes, inspector, it is. And a fine thing it is."

"A fine thing?"

Just down a little way from the inn's front stone steps is the path that leads to Peabury, sir."

We indeed found the White Hart and agreed to lodge there. Hawk and I had a lovely little room that overlooked the back of the inn. "I'm happy you followed us Hawkeye. Tomorrow shall prove to be an interesting day, I am sure of it."

❉ ❉ ❉

Early the next morning as we left the inn, I noticed the inspector had a gig waiting for us.

"Here we are then, Miss Wilson, step up, step up."

Being careful to keep my hem from becoming soiled on the step, I, at last, situated myself, but Hawkeye, not one to be left behind, hastily jumped onto my lap, dust and all.

Inspector Palgrave just shook his head as he gathered the

reins of the one-horse skip, and off we were to Peabury in a flurry.

"It's a lovely walk, sir. I've done it many times."

"Well, I'm happy for you, Miss Wilson. However, a Scotland Yard man should arrive with official aplomb." He glanced over at me. "You do understand?"

Official aplomb? "Oh, indeed, sir."

* * *

Arriving under the carriage-porch at Peabury, we were met by one of the servants. "I do not recognise him, sir."

"No matter." The inspector stepped from the gig and helped me down.

By then, a stable boy had approached to secure the horse. This time I recognised someone, it was Rufus. He was the kind young man who helped me with Sugar, but I could tell by the way he glanced me over that he did not remember me at all.

"Sir, may I inform the butler that you have come to call?"

Palgrave handed him his card. "I have come to speak with Lord Sheffield."

Rufus nodded. "Please, sir, come this way." He escorted us into the parlour where we were told to take a seat. "I will return shortly, sir."

We heard footfalls, subdued male voices, a few doors closing, and then within a very short time Mr Buffle entered. If he recognised me, he didn't let on. Detective Palgrave stood.

"Sir, I am Mr Buffle, the butler. How may I help you?"

I remained sitting, quite out of the way of the two men.

"Yes, I am Detective Palgrave, Scotland Yard. I would like a private word with you ... before I summon the others."

Mr Buffle half-bowed, his stoic face remained without a single wrinkle, excepting the rise of his brows. "Very well, sir." He turned and headed for the door. "This way, Detective Palgrave."

I put my ear to the door to make sure they were gone before I opened it. The way to the kitchen was through the back stairs, and I wanted to find Bessy. I found the kitchen near deserted except for a scullery maid scrubbing the larder box. "Sara, where is everybody?"

She dropped her rag. "Oh, for me life, Grace, what be you doing here?" She glanced me up and down. "Wearing them fancy clothes and all."

"I've come to speak with Bessy and her ladyship."

"Oh, they sent Bessy away."

My heart sank. "Oh, dear me, where?"

"Moorgate, there's a big ball there tonight, Grace. You knowed she be a good scrubber."

I nodded. "Is everyone gone?"

"Everybody, we be having a nice peaceful time of it here, Grace." She straightened, took in a breath and held her back. "No running after his lordship at every ring."

"Why are they having a ball at Moorgate, Sara?"

"Oh, Lord Allenton is marrin' somebody."

I gaped. "Lord Allenton?"

Just then the door swung open. "Excuse me, Miss Wilson," said Mr Buffle, "but the inspector is waiting for you in the parlour."

I felt my face tighten and burn as I stood straight. "Oh, well, yes, thank you Mr Buffle." He turned to escort me. "No need, sir. I know the way."

"Of course you do."

I found Inspector Palgrave standing in the parlour reading some papers. "Sir, I just found that everyone, including my dear old Bessy, has gone to Moorgate and ..."

"Yes, I know." He folded the papers and put them in his vest pocket. "We shall leave immediately."

"Are we returning to Croydon, then?"

"No, we shall be attending the ball."

Chapter 13 – The Truth Be Told

We hurried away in our little gig, Hawkeye remained tightly lodged between the inspector and me. I sensed that he sensed something was to befall us, but I am not at all sure if it be good or evil. He remained snuggled between the two of us and never left our side the entire way—except only to do his business in the bush. We had journeyed nearly two hours when I inquired of the inspector. "Sir, do you know the way to Moorgate?"

Turning onto a well maintained pebbled drive, he gestured with his head. "There, Miss Wilson, is Moorgate."

Dusk was settling lavender about the wooded glen. In front of the brownstone mansion lay a water scene. Soft white clouds of orange and pink reflected in the tall windows as we approached. Birds flittered about the greenish water; the air was beginning to cool. Many fine coaches had gathered near the carriage-porch, fancy and shiny, their horses pawing the ground. Those inside their grand and elegant carriages ignored us as the inspector deftly swerved this way and that in our gig and then finally pulled up near what I supposed to be the servants' quarters.

"Lovely house, sir." I glanced down at Hawkeye. "Don't you think so, ol' boy?"

The inspector tied the reins. "Well, here we are then, at long last," he sighed.

"Sir, allow me to say I am not at all sure who this *new* Lord Allenton is. Dr Moore, the younger son, told me his brother and mother left for America years ago and that he sold his title, that is if you can imagine such a thing." I sat upright as if a jolt of lightning struck nearby. "Sir, perhaps somebody did purchase his lordship's title ..."

"No, I think not, Miss Wilson."

"Then are we to simply walk into the ballroom uninvited, sir?"

"I need no invitation, Miss Wilson."

"Oh, of course not, inspector, but what about me? What about Hawk?"

"Hawk will gladly stay behind and guard the gig while we are gone."

I nodded. "Oh, yes, he can do that very well." Noticing the well-dressed and important people climbing from their carriages, I settled back into my seat and took a great breath. "Oh, sir, I don't know ..."

Patting my shoulder, the inspector smiled. "Now then, Miss Wilson, just slip your little hand onto my arm, lift your pert little nose in the air and proceed along as if the Queen had insisted that you were to attend."

The Queen? "Very well, sir, but what if Her Majesty is here? I dare not snub her."

He shook his head as he climbed from the gig. A stable boy took the horse, wary of Hawkeye, as he proceeded with caution. Finding the entrance, we were met with stares by the other guests. I knew the look all too well. "By my word, Inspector, I have never seen so many jewels, furs, shiny silk dresses swishing about in my entire life. Why, it is quite intoxicating, sir."

"Intoxicating? Dear me, Miss Wilson, do not stagger about. Imagine the humility I would have to endure."

I laughed so loud I heard Hawkeye bark.

Gentlemen were dressed in black and white, their boots shiny and well-polished—impenetrable to any sort of mud and rain, at least. "They remind me of penguins, sir."

"And how would you know that?"

I shrugged. "Very good question, sir."

Very much laughter filled the air. Hmm's, ooh's and ah's came from every direction, filling the great room with little more than forced, trite triviality. Candlelight flickered high and low. Servants were scurrying about carrying trays of glasses full of sparkling white bubbles spiralling up, bursting at the brim. I was not at all sure exactly what it was. The smell of body odours mixed with lavender invaded my nose. "Sir, dare we stand in line?"

Just as the words floated off my tongue we were approached by a rather self-important looking sort of man-servant, I supposed. Looking down his nose at the inspector, he hemmed, "Sir, perhaps you and your guest have come to the wrong assembly."

"And who might you be?" replied Palgrave as he handed him his card.

With a quick glance at the Scotland Yard emblem, he nodded. "Inspector Palgrave, I am the butler, Mr Brown. Come this way, sir."

We were escorted past the receiving line and down a rather

lengthy hall and situated in what I thought might have been a library.

"His Lordship will be with you shortly, sir."

Inspector Palgrave nodded. "That is a very good thing, Mr Brown." He hemmed, "I am not one to be kept waiting."

The butler's face turned a twinge pink. "No, sir, I should think not." He bowed and left the room closing the door ever so quietly in our faces.

"Well, you told him, Inspector." I nodded. "You are very brave, sir. I could never sass a butler."

"Sass? I did nothing of the sort, Miss Wilson. I just set the tone."

Tone?

"Yes, Scotland Yard is not to be trifled with, not by even a lord, let alone a butler."

I silently clapped my hands. "Oh, so good of you, sir, I would love to be a detective, but I would imagine women are not allowed such a position."

"Well, you seem to be a very determined young lady, perhaps you'll become the first."

"Not with my imprisonment, sir."

"But, you are innocent of all charges, Miss Wilson."

My jaw dropped. "Innocent, sir? Is that your personal opinion or do you know something you are not sharing with me?"

"All in due time, Miss Wilson—do not get too far ahead of yourself."

"Oh, indeed, sir." I rubbed my stomach. "I am famished, sir. We must have passed the kitchen stairwell for I did smell something delicious. I would suppose Bessy is there right this minute." I took a seat and scooted back in it. "Lovely chair, sir." He took a seat next to me.

When the door opened the butler entered, and we stood.

"Sir, his lordship wishes to see you in the ballroom."

"No, that will not do, bring his lordship here." He withdrew his pocket-watch. "I will not be kept waiting a minute more. Do you understand, Mr Brown?"

"Indeed I do, sir." He bowed his way from the room.

"Oh, sir, they have provoked you, I can see that."

Palgrave took my elbow. "Did you say Bessy would be in the kitchen?"

"Yes, sir."

"Good. Now, go to her and bring her here."

He held the door. "Hurry away now, Miss Wilson and do as

I say."

I scurried down into the kitchen and found Bessy peeling potatoes. "Oh, Bessy, I am so relieved to have found ..."

"Excuse me, madam, is there something I may do for you?"

She was, apparently, the housekeeper. I could spot one in an instant.

Bessy stood, her lapful of potatoes tumbled about the floor. "Oh, Mrs Hulme, this be Lady Grace, London. Beg pardon, but she speakin' to me for ..."

With a dismissive wave, I grabbed Bessy's hand. "We must be going. Good evening Mrs Hulme. "Come along now, Bessy. I need you." I pulled her to my side. "Follow me."

Glancing back over her shoulder Bessy squirmed. "Where'd we be going in such a flash, Grace?"

"Remember Inspector Palgrave, Scotland Yard?"

"No," she grunted.

"Well, no time for explaining now, but he instructed me to find you and bring you to the library." We flew up the servant's staircase and near ran down the hall. "So, I am Lady Grace is it?"

"You be fine as any of 'em here, Gracie. Where'd we be going?"

"To a room full of books stacked wall to ceiling, I think they call it the library."

"Well, I dunno about that, I rarely get out of the kitchen what with peeling this, scrubbing that ..."

When we reached the library door, I could hear male voices. We entered quietly. Inspector Palgrave nodded to me as we tiptoed around him trying to find the most inconspicuous place possible. Once settled, and with little noise, I glanced about the room. "Bessy," I whispered, "who is that portly gentleman standing by the hearth?"

"Lord Allenton, I dunno the other."

"Lord Allenton? How is that so, Bessy?" I whispered.

"Well, now that his father is dead, that be his son, Master George, the new Lord Allenton."

My heart sank—the dear old Lord Allenton was dead? "How do you know, Bessy?" I whispered.

She shrugged.

"And I thought Lord Allenton's son and wife were in America." I stared at the *new* lordship and couldn't find any resemblance to his father or his brother, Dr Moore. This man was much taller, with sandy-brown thinning hair, portly, and with dark eyes and a much louder, commanding tone.

Just then, the door opened and a lady swirled in—her shoulder-length black ringlets bounced about her bare shoulders. She wore a shiny red satin evening gown and moved about the room as if she owned the place. Her dark eyes sparkling like her diamond necklace. She stopped in the middle of the room, in quite a flourish, I might add. Bessy and I drew back in awed wonder.

"Sir, what is the meaning of this?" she said to the inspector.

She spoke English, but not the sort of accent I could readily make sense of. "Bessy," I whispered, "who's that lady?"

"I dunno."

She must have heard us whispering and turned. Glaring, she huffed, "And who might you two be? And what are you doing shirking there in the corner?"

Bessy dropped her paring knife.

I squared my shoulders and lifted my nose in the air. "Madam, we are not shirking, I assure you, we are merely ..."

"Miss Wilson," interrupted the inspector, "please return to your seat—and take Miss Bennett with you." He returned his attention to the woman in red. "I presume you are Lady Allenton?"

She shifted her stance with a lift to her chin, no doubt mimicking my pose. "Soon to be," she said with such an air, "and just who might you be?"

Lord Allenton hurried to her side and in a muffled whisper said, "Now, dear, there is quite a misunderstanding. You must calm yourself."

"Calm myself, and why should I do that and who are these people?"

Palgrave hemmed, "Madam, I am from Scotland Yard. I have a few questions to ask ..."

"Well, you will just have to come back in the morning. Cannot you see we are in the midst of a grand ball? We are to be married tomorrow."

Palgrave's face reddened. "Actually, madam, I do not care if you were in the middle of a royal wedding procession at Westminster Abby. I will have my questions answered here and now. Have I made myself quite clear, madam?"

Her face puckered red. "Well, I have never ..."

The inspector eyed Lord Allenton. "We have not been properly introduced, sir."

"Well, I'll have you know I am Lord Allenton."

Palgrave looked him over. "Oh, yes, the very reason I am here. So, your given name is George Moore. Is that right, sir?"

"Yes, that's right, Earl of Allenton. Why do you ask?"

The so-called bride-to-be looked on with an air of indignation. One brow arched much higher than the other. Her rouged lips puckered, her bouncy little ringlets dangling about her bare shoulders. "Really now, inspector, how cunning of you to have solved such a stupid little game of names, but you seemed to have missed mine. I'll have you know I am Miss Amelia Astoriff, New York. You do know where New York is, sir? Well, at any rate, I do hope you are quite through with your questioning." She tossed her black lace evening cape over her shoulder and started for the door. "Good evening, I must return to my guests."

"Take a seat, madam. I am not done with you yet."

She turned and glared at the inspector. My heart was beating madly in my chest. How dare she sass the inspector.

"George, are you just going to stand there and let that man speak to me in such a tone?"

"Amelia, please do calm yourself." Lord Allenton turned to the inspector. "Now, my good man, what is all this business about?"

The inspector turned to me. "Miss Wilson, please come to my side."

I nodded. "Indeed, sir."

Bessy stood stone quiet, I noticed a few potato peelings had stuck to her soiled apron. She kept her head low, her hands behind her back.

"May Bessy join us, inspector?"

"Oh, indeed, she may."

Bessy backed up and hit the wall. "Oh, me just stay here."

"No, no, do join us, Bessy," said Palgrave motioning for her to come.

Miss Astoriff sneered. "Oh, George, how am I to bear such incivility. I thought you told me you were a rich Englishman, an Earl with vast holdings," she huffed. "Why, how can you allow such ... "

"No need to fret Miss Astoriff," said Palgrave, "just take a seat over there." He gestured. "Do make yourself comfortable, the evening is yet begun."

The inspector held an odd sort of look, a half-grin – a smile, a sneer? Well, I was not at all sure just what was traversing through his brain, but I remained steady by his side with Bessy now steady at my side—I took her trembling hand.

Palgrave turned to his lordship. "You may join your bride-to-be."

He did just that, but his bride-to-be's frosty glare positioned him at arm's length.

Now standing at the open door commanding the attention of all those within, the inspector said, "I shall return shortly. In the meantime, no one is to leave this room."

"May we take a seat, or shall we remain standing like idiotic morons?" asked Miss Astoriff with a sneer.

"Idiots stand, morons sit. Do as you wish." He closed the door with a thud.

Staring after the door, his lordship shook his head. "I shall have a word with the Chief Superintendent at the Met over this entire matter and particularly this so-called Inspector Palgrave—such a nerve." Cocking his head, he tilted his ear toward the front of the house. "What is that I hear?" He sauntered to the window and looked out. "Why, our guests are leaving." Shaking his head in apparent disgust, he rejoined Miss Astoriff. "What a disgrace this inspector has brought upon Moorgate ..."

"Disgrace?" she said, "it's more than a disgrace, George. How shall we get married under such a cloud? And what, pray tell, are you hiding that requires the need of a Scotland Yard detective snooping about?"

"Me?" his lordship took such a look, nervously packing his pipe. "Perhaps, madam, it is you whom he chooses to question. Why, certainly not me. I have done nothing wrong."

Miss Astoriff glared at Bessy and me. "Well then, it must involve you two urchins. What have you done?" She singled out Bessy. "You no doubt stole silver or ..." she clutched the diamond necklace at her throat, "... my precious jewellery! They had better be wrapped and secured in my room as I have left them." She chided his lordship. "*If* I marry you sir, I will bring my own housekeeper. She will put this sloppy household in proper order within the week, depend upon it." She returned her frosty glare to us both. "And in regards to you ..."

Up came Bessy's chin. "I never stole nothing in me whole life, you old crow."

Just then the door opened, and inspector Palgrave entered. "Well, you chose to remain standing I see."

Miss Astoriff sauntered to the red velvet sofa and sat. "Get on with it inspector, please do." Fluttering her lace fan in the air, she glanced at us. "Arrest those two thieves and be done with it."

Palgrave looked at me and smiled. "Those two have done nothing wrong, Miss Astoriff from New York."

"Well then inspector what is all this about?" said his lordship tapping his smouldering pipe into its amber coloured glass bowl.

"I have dismissed your guests and summoned Mr O'Malacy and Mr Buffle to join us."

His lordship looked down his nose. "I have no recent memory of a Mr O'Malacy. Mr Buffle, of course, is my personal man-servant. What possible need are we of those two, inspector? What the devil is going on? I demand to know."

"They will be escorted here shortly, your lordship."

"Escorted?" said Lady Astoriff with such a tone. "Escorted by whom?"

"I am quite confident my Scotland Yard colleagues are up to the job, madam."

Crossing her arms in a huff, she held a sour look as she squirmed back into the overstuffed, green and white striped wing-chair. "I must see this for myself."

"Oh, believe me, madam, you shall," said the inspector.

Just then the door opened, and a nurse pushed a wheelchair into the room, Lady Allenton quickly followed. I couldn't believe my eyes, there in the chair looking quite sprite was Lord Allenton himself, the very man beaten and sent away years ago. I hurried to his side. "Oh, sir, that you are alive and well?"

His head was a little droopy, but he managed to take my hand. Squinting up into my eyes, he smiled. "Poppy?"

"Oh, indeed it is, sir."

I heard his son gasp. "Father ... why, what has become of you?" He hurried to his side. "Why ... why, we thought you had died, years ago."

Lady Allenton glared at her son. "You are a disgraceful brute, George. All along you lied and deceived us." She bent down and kissed his lordship's shiny little bald head. "Imagine such a despicable trick sending your father to Australia to rot in a prison." Holding her hands over his lordship's ears, she sighed in a most dramatic manner, swooning greatly. "Dearest, I will spare you his lies. There is no end to them, it seems."

Her son glared at her. "Remove your hands, Mother." He positioned himself in front of his father. "Yes, Father, Mother is right, there is no end to the lies—all of our lies. I admit it and quite frankly, I am relieved that this charade is over." He held out his hands to Inspector Palgrave. "Sir, I am at your disposal."

Miss Astoriff stood. "George, what have you done?" She glanced at the elder Lord Allenton. "This old man is your father? I thought he was dead." She took in a great breath. "That means you are not a Lord anymore? And I won't be a lady?"

"You ain't no lady anyways," cackled Bessy, "and me hopes you goes back to New York yesterday."

"Oh, your lordship," I took his shrivelled little hand and held it to my cheek, "I am so sorry you had to endure this."

He hung his little head and wept into my handkerchief. "Oh, I never believed my intuition about them. Once gone, I never imagined I would ever see my beloved Moorgate again."

His rheumy eyes moistened, but held the sparkly blue neath his droopy lids.

Lady Allenton took my hand. I could not mistake the desperation in her grip, nor the look of consternation on her face. "Oh, young lady," she whispered, "you *must* use your influence with the Inspector and have the charges against me dropped ... he is in love with you, and I am, after all your ...."

Inspector Palgrave stepped between us and firmly dislodged her hand from mine. I was stunned at such a rude gesture. Did he actually think her ladyship was involved in such a dastardly affair? And what did she mean by saying he was in love with me? What a preposterous assertion. I glanced at the inspector's red and twisted face. He was very angry.

"Lady Allenton," he fumed, "save your begging for the magistrate." He turned to me. "Miss Wilson, I would wish it of you to take a seat now." He glanced at Bessy. "Miss Bennett, take Miss Wilson's hand and guard her."

Bessy hurried to my side and put her arm around me. "Nobody be harmin' me Grace, sir."

I glanced up into the inspector's face. "Sir?"

"Be patient Miss Wilson."

At his words I heard the door open and who should enter but Mr O'Malacy, the very policeman who arrested me and his lordship years ago. I hardly recognised the swinish man for he was not in his uniform. However, I could not mistake the curly black hair, cruel eyes, the down-turned lips, and his protruding belly—though it had dropped considerably.

His lordship buried his head in his hands and moaned.

Approaching Inspector Palgrave, O'Malacy grunted, "Where'd you want me?"

"Stand next to George Moore," said the inspector. "I'm most certain you know the man."

Indeed, I thought, *he'll not stand next to me.*

George's eyes widened as the man approached, whispering something to him from the corner of his mouth, but I could not make it out. George hastily poured himself a drink, but instead of sipping it casually, he gulped it down and poured another.

"That will do, Mr Moore," said the inspector as he took the bottle from George and set it atop the mantle ledge next to the clock. "You'll need to keep your wits about you this evening. That is, what's left of them."

I was beginning to piece together thoughts of their debauchery when the door opened again. A gentleman emerged.

Bessy nudged me. "He's come back, Grace."

"You know him?"

"Aye, that be Mr Cooke."

I shook my head. I was not at all sure it was really him. "It's been so long, Bessy. I hardly recognised him."

His lordship sat up, stiff and quite proper. With an odd sort of smile, he nodded. "Mr Cooke, so glad you could join us this evening."

Mr Cooke stood straight-backed, dressed in immaculate black jacket and trousers. His cologne filled the air with mint. He half-bowed. "Indeed, sir."

"Again, I must say I have not been attended to in so fine a manner as you did evening last, Mr Cooke. I am more than pleased to find you in health and have come back to me."

"Thank you, sir." Cooke's face settled into a fine, self-assured countenance. He half-bowed again. "It was an honour, to again, serve you, sir. Now, if you will excuse me, sir."

"Oh, indeed, Mr Cooke, indeed." His lordship waved him off with his frail, scaly, pink little hand.

Mr Cooke approached the inspector. "Sir, good evening, so nice to see you again so soon after meeting." He scanned the faces of George Moore and O'Malacy with a deep frown.

"Indeed, Mr Cooke," said Palgrave, "now, I would wish it of you to stand very near his lordship."

"With pleasure, sir." With a curt bow, Mr Cooke joined his lordship. Bessy and I remained sitting at his left.

Without a knock, the door opened, and Lord Sheffield and his wife entered. I smiled, but she did not yet find me. Glancing nervously about the room, she finally caught my eye and came to my side. "Oh, Grace, I was assured you would be here, and I am glad." She patted my hand. "Be brave my dear girl, be brave."

Be brave? "Oh, ma'am, I am not the one to be brave, it is Lord Allenton who is to be pitied, for I do not know what calamity is yet to come."

"Neither do I."

Lord Sheffield approached the inspector. With his monocle

situated in his left eye he squinted. "Well done, inspector, well done." Glancing at his wife, he gestured with his hand. "Look there Catherine, George is just there, your sister repugnant as usual. Inspector, why are they not in chains?"

"So much to do in so little time, my lord. I do pray you have it in your heart to forgive the oversight." Palgrave positioned himself at the doorway. "Lord Sheffield, you must remember Mr Cooke, Lord Allenton's butler for many years, and there, standing next to your nephew is Mr O'Malacy, once a policeman in London. Mr Buffle will soon be brought amongst us."

Lord Sheffield's brow knit as he looked them all over. "But of course, Inspector Palgrave, I am acquainted with them all, except the policeman. Am I to suppose that I should be happy that I have never made *his* acquaintance?"

"Right you are, sir."

At the finish of his words, who should enter the room but Buffle himself. This time his self-assuredness was not quite so grand. His forehead was beaded with perspiration, his cravat stained yellowish and frayed. He closed the door quietly behind him and half-bowed at Inspector Palgrave. "I have been summoned, escorted, if you will, sir."

Inspector Palgrave nodded. "Escorted, indeed. Have you any idea why, Mr Buffle?"

He glanced around the room and noticeably rested his gaze upon O'Malacy and George Moore's faces. "Well, I suppose so, sir."

"Go on, Mr Buffle or should I say, Mr Bigley?"

Suddenly Buffle's face lost its red glow, his chest sank. He seemed to become befuddled. "Well, I ..."

Lady Sheffield nudged me and whispered, "I found out who gave you the money, Grace."

"Oh, indeed, your ladyship, will you tell me?"

Before answering, she glanced over at George, O'Malacy and Buffle. She shook her head and whispered, "All of them vile creatures, to be sure—including my dear sister."

My mouth dropped. "Your sister, ma'am? But, what has *she* done?"

"Ringleader, and might I add ..."

"My dear, do hush your voice," chided Lord Sheffield to his wife. "This is no time for gossip."

She smiled down into my eyes. "My dearest husband confessed to me of his generosity to you, Grace, the animal girl ..."

"He gave me the money, ma'am?"

She nodded. "Your 'adoring' friend, Dr Moore, had words with my husband regarding your circumstances, Poppy. Moreover, his lordship said you made me 'well again' and wanted you to come back to Peabury."

"Oh, dear me, I can hardly understand a bit of it."

Her ladyship put her arm around my waist. "Be brave my dear. I will only be a few feet away, come what may."

Come what may? What could she mean? I swallowed hard. "Very well, madam."

The room, by now, was near full. Standing near the window stood George Moore and O'Malacy. Lord Allenton sat quiet and still in his cane chair with wheels, while Mr Cooke stood erect and proper at his side. Bessy and I stood to his lordship's left. Lady Allenton with a sullen gaze remained motionless, staring at the floor. Inspector Palgrave still held a most severe look.

A timid knock came upon the door.

"Come," he called out.

Entering slowly and holding her head low, came a lady painted with much rouge and wax ... surely of late middle age. Her thick black ringlets dangled a few inches below her hand-made bonnet of straw—a few silk flowers resembling bluebells about its brim. Her eyes never left Mr Cooke's.

"That's right, Margaret," said Mr Cooke, "you will stand next to me."

She curtsied to his lordship and then took her place next to Cooke, never looking my way. When she removed her gloves, I was stunned to notice the very ring upon her wedding finger that Mr O'Malacy accused me of stealing—Mr Cooke's ring, the very one I was thrown in prison over. I was most certain it was the very one. Surely there could not be so many that I could be so easily mistaken. I looked her up and down. "Bessy," I whispered, "do you know her?"

"That be the woman Mr Cooke drove away with last year."

"Is she his wife then?"

She shrugged. "I dunno, Gracie."

"She looks ever so familiar, Bessy." I brushed away the dried potato skins from Bessy's apron and watched them scatter about the floor. I grabbed her hand before she could bend down to pick them up. "No matter, Bessy."

Then the door opened again and in came Dr Moore, my physician friend, Lord Allenton's youngest son. He stood for a second looking around the room. When he spied Mr Cooke's wife, he hurried to her side. "Well, well, if it isn't my old governess,

Miss Wilson?"

"Wilson?" I stepped forward. "Could there be two of us?"

Dr Moore turned at my voice. "Oh ..." he stammered, "Miss Wilson?"

"Yes, Dr Moore that is right." I hurried to his side. "It is very good to see you again, sir."

"Dr Moore," said Mr Cooke's wife, "we have recently wed, my name is no longer Wilson." She smiled at me and flashed the ring in my face. She then looked deep into my eyes. Suddenly she took hold of my chin, her thick rouged lips parted. Her breath carried a whiff of gin. "Poppy?"

Startled, for who should know my name in these circles? Inspector Palgrave was at my side in an instant. He held such a look I could not right off read it.

My head was spinning. "Yes, but ..."

"Look deep into my eyes, dear girl. Do you see something familiar dancing therein?"

As if a massive strike of lightning struck my brain, I caught my breath. Still I was not certain, for it had been many years. "Mama?"

Palgrave took my trembling hand.

"Mama?" I cried again at the uncertainty of this stranger.

He positioned himself between her and me. With a great snarl, he snapped, "Madam, henceforth, you will not work your charms on this innocent, sweet young lady. I absolutely forbid it."

The room grew very quiet, the only sound being Hawkeye as he scratched his way into the room sniffing this and that until finally at my side.

In a loud commanding voice, Inspector Palgrave called out for an Inspector Thomas, who came from around the drapes, hidden there miraculously, I declare.

"Arrest them all, Thomas."

Soon the room was full of Scotland Yard police.

"Under what charges, exactly," said Mrs Cooke now putting her attention onto Allenton's eldest son, George. "Indeed, Inspector Palgrave and what charges will be levelled at *him*, I ask. Years ago he had his way with me," tossing her head in defiance, she shouted, "yes, I planned it all, and now I will have my way with *him!*" She laughed. "And I'll live to see him pay the price."

The blood drained from Mr Cooke's face. Seething, he glared at his wife. "I knew you couldn't keep your mouth shut, Margaret!"

The elder Lord Allenton glanced up from his chair. "The

charges? Attempted murder, theft of my personal belongings, absconding with my fortune," he dropped his head, "leaving me in utter ruin—the Allenton name forever disgraced."

Lord Sheffield approached and lay his hand upon his brother-in-law's shoulder. "No, John, your honour is above reproach. In time, your good name will regain its lustre. Her Majesty has personally assured me of it. What is more, you will not be left in ruin." He sniffed the air. "I simply would not allow it."

Lady Sheffield put her arms around me. "Lest we forget Miss Grace Wilson who was wrongly incarcerated for twelve years—innocent of the charges, so deemed by the Queen, two days past." She knelt by my side. "Oh, dear Grace, I wanted to shield you from all this, but ..." she glanced at Palgrave, "we were sworn to secrecy."

Dr Moore smiled over at me as he tended his father. "That's right, Cousin, we couldn't say a word."

Cousin? My lips parted, confusion obviously written plain as day upon my face. "Cousin?"

Inspector Palgrave smiled.

Lord Sheffield held a grim look as he glared at his nephew George. "Indeed, let it be known to all, I disown you, George Moore. Good riddance to you and your ridiculous mother, scoundrels that you are! I hope you all rot in prison."

Patting Hawkeye's little head, Palgrave nodded. "I will personally see to it, your lordship." With one arm, he tenderly took my hand and led me to the sofa. Sitting very near me, he situated Hawkeye onto his lap. Dr Moore tucked a day blanket about his father and gently pushed him to our side. Lord Allenton held a kind smile toward me, he had been weeping. I dabbed away the tears with my handkerchief. Lady Sheffield and Lord Sheffield hovered around us as well. Dear Bessy, looking terribly out of place, crouched bravely at my feet, hugging my legs.

Watching as the police escorted the sordid crowd of crooks from the room, I shuddered at the thought: "Why, I rather supposed that wretched woman was my mother." I sighed deeply. "She looked so familiar—goodness me, what a dreadful mistake I could have made thinking she was my own." Tears sprung to my eyes and dripped freely upon Palgrave's hand. "I thought at long last I had found her ..."

He squeezed my hand. "My dear Miss Wilson, that woman *was* your mother."

Chapter 14 – Mrs Palgrave and the Ring

An interesting four years have passed since discovering my mother, or should I say rediscovering her. I have not the heart, nor desire to visit her, though my good husband encourages me to do so. 'Forgiveness, my dear, heals the heart.' I would answer, "Oh, yes, I know. Perhaps tomorrow then ..."

As I sit here in the morning room, I reflect back now and again of smelling prison stench on a passer-by and taking my husband's hand. "Oh, Peter, I cannot forgive her." He would calmly answer, "Perhaps tomorrow ..."

"I beg your pardon, Mrs Palgrave, but there is an early caller." Horace, our man-servant, held out the mail salver. "Her card, madam."

I stood and examined it. "I do not recognise the name, Horace." I hurried to the window and looked out. "Well, I must say her carriage looks very fine; the horses not come into a sweat." I glanced back at the card. "Very well then, send her in. Where is Mr Palgrave, by the way?"

"Off to the office very early this morning, ma'am."

"Oh, yes, I see. Well, how is the lady dressed?"

"Somewhat fine, ma'am—certainly not rich, however." Horace squared his shoulders. "And ma'am, that is not *her* carriage." He pulled the curtain aside and pointed down the street. "There awaits her cart, with a donkey."

"A donkey cart?" I smiled with a sigh. "There was many a day I prayed for such a cart."

He nodded. "Indeed, ma'am."

"Very well, send her in. And please, bring my spectacles."

"Indeed, ma'am."

I took my usual chair by the hearth and listened as Horace escorted the woman into our home. I sniffed the air quite certain it was filled with apple spice, the hearth fire pleasant—the room warm and inviting. A light knock and they entered.

I stood. The woman was indeed dressed in a very modest, but neat muslin day dress. Her dark hair twisted up and fastened with a tortoise comb. Her tiny black feathered hat sat cocked to the side, feathers poking toward Hawkeye who remained asleep on the hearthrug. Her gloves, matching a small purse dangled at her side; she did not give off any odours of any sort.

Horace nodded and handed me my spectacles. "Will that be all, ma'am?"

"Yes, thank you."

I glanced at her card. "Forgive me, Mrs Andrews, but I do not recollect the occasion of our first meeting."

"Oh, Mrs Palgrave, we have never met. Forgive me the intrusion, but I come with news."

"News?" I couldn't imagine what this plain woman and I had in common that she was bringing *me* any sort of news. She looked well-weathered and without even a proper cape about her shoulders. "I take it you've travelled a great distance."

The stranger glanced down at her muddied hem and dung-caked boots. "Only from Newgate and Old Bailey, ma'am."

"All the same, quite a distance in this weather, but, do go on, Mrs Andrews."

"Your mother has died."

I must have looked somewhat stunned as I absentmindedly removed my glasses and sat. "I see."

"Your mother wanted me to give this to you." She withdrew from her purse a small black velvet pouch and set it on the side table next to me. "There you are, Mrs Palgrave." She smiled. "Well, I must be going."

"Mrs Cooke was my mother. You knew her, then, Mrs Andrews?"

"Ever so slightly, Mrs Palgrave, I knew her as Margaret Wilson Cooke."

"Yes, that was my maiden name, Wilson. Please, have a seat and explain your association with her. I am more than curious at your familiarity with my mother." I knew very little of her in the first place, and it was beyond my curiosity that a complete stranger should enter my home and deposit a gift of some sort claiming to know her. She did, however, know her maiden name and that lent credibility to her voice. I watched as she sat and fumbled with her drawstring purse. She withdrew a handkerchief and dabbed her nose.

I glanced at the black velvet pouch. "What is it?"

"Oh, ma'am, I do not know what is there."

I once more took note of her outfit. The frayed sleeves of her frock, her boots scuffed and near spent. "Will you be so kind as to tell me then how you came to own it and deliver it to me, Mrs Andrews?"

She looked up into the chandelier and then back down into my face. "Mrs Palgrave, I am a warden at the prison where your mother ... lived. She spoke kindly of you every day, I must say."

I doubt that.

"She was the exception, meaning she knew to write very well and speak properly."

"Yes, she was an educated young woman, very young—naive and innocent; a governess to Lord Allenton's eldest son at one time."

"Oh, yes, of course, I have heard the name."

"Indeed." Feeling a remnant of anxiety that used to haunt me, I took in a great breath. "Back then we were very poor, and I suppose one would do anything to survive," I straightened, "except of course abandon one's only child."

She nodded. "Unconscionable."

I knew I could speak openly with this woman, she, of course, probably knew my history as well. "At least Mother taught me to read and write, and that was what kept me from being molested while in prison." I stood, biting my lip. "You see, I was held on false charges."

"Yes, Mrs Palgrave, I know."

I looked deeply into her eyes. "Yes, I suppose you would."

"Days before your mother died, she made me promise to deliver that pouch to you."

We both glanced at it as it sat on the table—a soft black velvet blur of cloth with its black satin strings tied neatly in a tiny bow.

Picking it up, I pulled open the strings, and a ring slid into my lap. Mrs Andrews gasped at its brilliance; the large diamond sparkled greatly under the chandelier. The years-old patina of silver glistened even still.

"Oh, dear me, Mrs Palgrave I had no idea ..."

"Do you have children, Mrs Andrews?"

She smiled. "Oh, yes, Mrs Palgrave, I have three boys yet alive and two girls death-born."

"A husband?"

"No, ma'am, he died in the coal pits last year. The walls collapsed ... " Her lips pursed.

"Yes, I have heard of such dangers. I am very sorry to hear it." I stood, sliding the ring back into the little pouch. "Well, Mrs Andrews, I am blessed with a good husband and a good life." I took her hand and placed the pouch into her palm and closed her fingers around it. "Take it. I have no need of its memories."

She looked startled, her jaw dropped.

"And my dear, no worries, it is an honest piece of jewellery." I hugged her. "Go now, your children will miss you."

"Oh, Mrs Palgrave, I cannot take it."

"Oh, sell it and live comfortably ever after." I handed her my card. "If anyone questions you about it, mention my husband's name—he is Superintendent at Scotland Yard. You'll not have any troubles."

"Sell it?" She looked perplexed.

"Oh, it is worth a fortune, to be sure."

"But, ma'am what about you?"

"Me? Did not my mother tell you who my father was?"

"No."

"She was impregnated by Lord Allenton's eldest son, George," I said with a deep sigh. "And I suppose not to her liking for she spent many years planning her retribution, owing to her ruin. Lord Allenton was my grandfather, bless his now-departed soul. No, Mrs Andrews, I have no need for money. I am wealthy enough with two healthy sons and a very dear husband."

Hawkeye was now awake and sitting at my feet. I knelt down and kissed the top of his little head. "Oh, my darling little man, how I adore you."

My heart felt, for the first time in many years, light with painless sorrows. Forgiveness indeed heals the heart, but I out-waited forgiveness owing to time and the thought of tomorrow as today's needless concern.

"Indeed," I took in a deep, satisfying breath, "I feel like a little bird perched at an open window." Taking her trembling hand, I smiled warmly. "Thank you, Mrs Andrews, delivering such bad news must be difficult. Goodbye now, and may God's blessings visit you often."

Other Great Novels by this Author

Winthrope – *Tragedy to Triumph*
The Arrangement – *Love Prevails*
Bobbin's Journal – *Waif to Wealth*
Poppy – *The Stolen Family*
Sophie & Juliet – *Rags to Royalty*
The Spinster – *Worth the Wait*
Holybourne – *The Magic of a Child*

A Novel Victorian Cookbook – *Forgotten Gems*

Cookbook

Be sure to check out Carol's newest addition to her historical novel collection – *A Novel Victorian Cookbook*. Characters from all seven novels describe their favourite meals. Imagine creating your own Victorian dinner party for family and friends and while they dine, entertain them with stories of your favourite characters.

Slipcases

The author also has created hand-painted slipcases to house her collection of seven novels. Each one is a unique, numbered collector's item.

Paintings

After encouraging artistic reviews of her slipcases, the author has branched out to painting on canvas and wood, in the style of 19th century painters. You can see some of her work on her website.

Links and Reviews

Visit the author's website: KennedyLiterary.com
Like on Facebook: caroljeannekennedy
Follow on Twitter @carol823599

www.ingramcontent.com/pod-product-compliance
Lightning Source LLC
Chambersburg PA
CBHW050541190726
48284CB00003B/1166